Blood and Mistletoe

Also by E.J. Stevens

Spirit Guide
Young Adult Series

She Smells the Dead
Spirit Storm
Legend of Witchtrot Road
Brush with Death
The Pirate Curse

Ivy Granger World

Ivy Granger
Urban Fantasy Series

Shadow Sight
Blood and Mistletoe
Ghost Light
Club Nexus
Burning Bright
Birthright
Hound's Bite (2016)

Hunters' Guild
Urban Fantasy Series

Hunting in Bruges
Hunting in Paris (2016)

Dark Arcana
Urban Fantasy Series

The Magician (TBA)

IVY GRANGER PSYCHIC DETECTIVE

Blood and Mistletoe

E.J. STEVENS

Published by Sacred Oaks Press
Sacred Oaks, 221 Sacred Oaks Lane, Wells, Maine 04090

First Printing (trade paperback edition), October 2015

Stevens, E.J.
Blood and Mistletoe / E.J. Stevens

ISBN 978-0-9894887-6-1 (trade pbk.)

Printed in the United States of America

PRONUNCIATION GUIDE

Pronunciations are given phonetically for names and races found in *Shadow Sight* and *Blood and Mistletoe*, the first novel and novella of the Ivy Granger series. Alternate names and nicknames have been provided in parentheses. In some cases, the original folklore has been changed to suit the city of Harborsmouth and its environs.

Athame: *ah-thaw-may*
Barguest: *bar-guyst* (Bargheist, Black Dog)
Blaosc: *blee-usk*
Brownie: *brow-nee* (Bwca, Urisk, Hearth Faerie, Domestic Hobgoblin)
Bugbear: *bug-bayr* (Bug-a-boo, Boggle-bo)
Bwca: *bu-ka* (see Brownie)
The Cailleach: *kall-ahk* (The Blue Hag, Cailleach Bheur, Queen of Winter, Crone, Veiled One, Winter Hag)
Cat Sidhe: *kat shee* or *kayth shee* (Faerie Cat, Cait Shith, Cait Sith)
Ceffyl Dŵr: *Keff-eel Door* (Kelpie King)
Clurichaun: *kloor-ih-kon* (clobhair)
Daeva: *day-va*
Demon: *dee-mon*
Each Uisge: *erkh ooshka* (Water Horse)
Faerie: *fayr-ee* (Fairy, Sidhe, Fane, Wee Folk, The Gentry, People of Peace, Themselves, Sidhe, Fae, Fay, Good Folk)
Fear Dearg: *far dar-rig* (The Red Man)
Forneus: *Fore-nee-uss* (Demon, Great Marquis of Hell)
Galliel: *Gal-ee-el* (Unicorn)
Ghoul: *gool* (Revenant)
Glaistig: *glass-tig* (The Green Lady)
Griffin: *griff-in* (Gryphon, Griffon)
Grindylow: *grin-dee-loh*
Hamadryad: *ha-ma-dry-ad* (Tree Nymph)
Hippocampus: *hip-po-cam-pus*
Hob-o-Waggle *Hob-oh-wag-l* (Brownie, son of Wag-at-the-Wa)

Jenny Greenteeth: *Jen-nee Green-teeth* (Water Hag)
Kelpie: *kel-pee* (Water Horse, Nyaggle)
Lamia: *lay-me-a*
Leanansídhe: *lan-awn-shee* (Lhiannan Sidhe, Leanhaun Shee,
Leannan Sìth, Fairy Mistress)
Leprechaun: *le-pre-khan* (leipreachán)
Mab: *Mab* (Unseelie Queen)
Melusine: *Mel-oo-seen*
Mermaid: *mer-mayd* (male Merman)
Merry Dancer: *mer-ree dan-ser* (Fir Chlis)
Murúch: *mer-ook* (Merrow, Moruadh, Murúghach)
Oberon: *O-ber-on* (Seelie King)
Peg Powler: *Peg Pow-ler* (Peg Powler of the Trees, Water Hag)
Peri: *per-ee*
Pixie: *pix-ee* (Pisgie)
Pooka: *poo-ka* (Phooka, Pouka, Púca, Pwca)
Redcap: *red-kap* (red cap)
Saytr: *say-tur*
Selkie: *sel-kee*
Shellycoat: *shell-ee-cote*
Sidhe: *shee* (see Faerie)
Succubus: *suk-you-bus* (male Incubus)
Titania: *Ti-tayn-ee-ah* (Seelie Queen)
Troll: *trol*
Tylwyth Teg: *till-with teeg* (Seelie Court)
Unicorn: *you-ne-korn*
Vampire: *vam-pi-r* (Undead)
Will-o-the-Wisp: *Wil-o-tha-Wisp* (Gyl Burnt Tayle, Jack o'
Lantern, Wisp, Ghost Light, Friar's Lantern, Corpse Candle,
Hobbledy, Aleya, Hobby Lantern, Chir Batti, Faerie Fire,
Spunkies, Min Min Light, Luz Mala, Pinket, Ellylldan, Spook
Light, Ignus Gatuus, Orbs, Boitatá, and Hinkypunk)

INTRODUCTION

Welcome to Harborsmouth, where monsters walk the streets unseen by humans…except those with second sight.

Whether visiting our modern business district or exploring the cobblestone lanes of the Old Port quarter, please enjoy your stay. When you return home, do tell your friends about our wonderful city—just leave out any supernatural details.

Don't worry—most of our guests never experience anything unusual. Otherworlders, such as faeries, vampires, and ghouls, are quite adept at hiding within the shadows. Many are also skilled at erasing memories. You may wake in the night screaming, but you won't recall why. Be glad that you don't remember—you are one of the fortunate ones.

If you do encounter something unnatural, we recommend the services of Ivy Granger, Psychic Detective. Co-founder of Private Eye detective agency, Ivy Granger is a relatively new member of our small business community. Her offices can be found on Water Street, in the heart of the Old Port.

Miss Granger has a remarkable ability to receive visions by the act of touching an object. This skill is useful in her detective work, especially when locating lost items. Whether you are looking for a lost brooch or missing persons, no job is too big or too small for Ivy Granger—but you may be on her waiting list for awhile. Hopefully you are not in dire need of her immediate services. After her role in recent events, where she was instrumental in saving our city, Miss Granger's business is booming.

If matters are particularly grim, we can also provide, upon request, a list of highly skilled undertakers. If you are in need of their services, then we also kindly direct you to Harborsmouth Cemetery Realty. It's never too early to contact them, since we have a booming "housing" market. Demand is quite high for a local plot—there are always people dying for a place to stay.

Happy holidays!

"If I could work my will," said Scrooge indignantly, "Every idiot who goes about with 'Merry Christmas' on his lips, should be boiled with his own pudding, and buried with a stake of holly through his heart."

—Charles Dickens, *A Christmas Carol*

CHAPTER 1

I woke to the smell of gingerbread and coffee. Too bad the two were one and the same.

"This is why I hate the holidays," I muttered into my cup. "Who messes around with a perfectly good cup of coffee?"

"You're just grumpy because Ceffyl stood you up last night," Jinx said.

"Well, it was a lame excuse," I said.

I dropped my gloved hands into my lap, staring through a sheet of sleep mussed hair at the snowmen that danced maniacally around my pajama pants. I was pouting. Damn, I never pout, but I had been excited about our date last night. Which in retrospect was silly—I hate Christmas.

But this was my first holiday season with a boyfriend and I had wanted to do all of the normal date stuff. Instead, I sat home and watched Rudolph the Red-Nosed Reindeer for the gazillionth time. Jinx had suggested wearing the Christmas pj's we'd exchanged as gifts last year. I traced the smiling snowmen with a gloved finger, wishing I could be that happy for once.

Ceff had promised to take me to the tree lighting in Fountain Square. I didn't like crowds, and usually avoided them like the plague, but Ceff had lured me with promises of hot chocolate and my weight in peppermint cookies. He also said he had a present for me.

My heart thumped and I shivered as chill fingers of fear and anticipation ran up my spine. What kind of gift would a kelpie king give me?

Would it be something pretty, romantic, practical, magical—would it drive me insane?

I discovered early in life that touching unknown objects could lead to terrifying visions. I was nine years old when my psychic gift reared its ugly, traumatizing head. I've been wary of receiving gifts ever since.

Strong emotions leave behind an imprint. People like me, with a talent for psychometry, can tap into that psychic imprint and see glimpses of an object or persons' past.

Psychometry requires physical contact, thank Mab. That's the reason why I wear gloves twenty-four-seven. It's definitely not a fashion statement—Jinx is the fashionista in this friendship. I had learned the hard way that covering my hands helped to keep me sane.

Too bad an impermeable, full body suit wasn't practical. In fact, it would be potentially fatal. I may be part fae, but my human half still has to breathe. Plus, Jinx would never let me leave our loft apartment dressed in a full body condom. That would be breaking too many fashion rules. Alas, I should have been a pooka.

"Pfft," Jinx said with a shrug. "Ceffyl is king of the kelpies, give the guy a break. I'm sure he isn't thrilled to be swimming in the freezing cold ocean while negotiating boring hunting treaties between kelpie and selkie tribes."

It was true. Ceffyl hadn't been happy about cancelling our date. He'd broken a length of wooden railing in frustration when the call came in.

*****

We'd been walking along the waterfront under the stars, our new favorite pastime, when Ceff had stopped to stare intently at the bay. Ceff leaned casually against the railing, but I could hear his teeth grinding over the lapping sound of the waves.

A head surfaced near the docks, bobbing like a fishing buoy on the gentle waves of the harbor. The water fae waved its webbed hands and began speaking to Ceff in a high pitched chatter that sounded similar to the squeaks and chirps of dolphin song. The words were unintelligible to my ears, but the message was clear. Ceff was needed elsewhere.

And when duty calls, kelpie kings have to listen. He wasn't happy about it. Storm clouds passed across Ceff's dark green eyes, making them shift to black, and he held the railing in a white knuckled grip.

Ceff nodded once toward the bay and, with a strange bobbing bow, the water fae messenger returned to the dark waters from which he came. Ceff continued to stare into the harbor as if he could alter the message the tides had brought him by will alone. I held my breath and waited.

"I regret that I must cancel our date for tomorrow evening," Ceff said.

His voice sounded calm, like a gentle burbling stream, but the shattered railing beneath his hands told another story.

"But it's the tree lighting," I said. "It only happens once a year. Can't they wait one day?"

"I'm afraid not," he said. "My people and a neighboring selkie tribe are both insistent that if they do not gain exclusive fishing rights over one small patch of ocean, then they will starve to death. It is foolishness, and I suspect the truth behind the dispute will have little to do with food supplies, but I must go before a small argument spirals into a war between the water fae. It is my duty."

"Do you really think they'd wind up killing each other over a patch of water and some fish?" I asked.

"Fae wars have been started over much less," he said. "But do not worry. Selkies are some of the most peaceful of our kind. I am sure I can negotiate a treaty and return before the Winter Solstice."

"Okay," I said lamely. "At least we can still make it to Kaye's solstice celebration."

"Yes," he said. "Have you enquired about the dress code? Witches can be very particular about their festivals and ritual gatherings, especially the eight annual Sabbats."

Kaye had mentioned the dress code for her party alright. I felt my face burn.

"Clothing is optional," I said. I shook my head. "I'm going to need therapy after this party, but Kaye has done a lot to help me over the past few months. I can't turn down her invitation."

"Madam O'Shaye has done much for us all," he said.

True, Kaye did help to save the entire city of Harborsmouth. The least we could do was attend her holiday ritual.

"Well, don't get too excited about the dress code," I said. "I'm wearing clothing. Not really a big fan of public nudity, or hypothermia."

"I can think of ways to keep warm," he said. His eyes smoldered, shifting from black to bright luminous green.

I took an involuntary step back. Not at Ceff's otherness, I actually thought his glowing eyes were sexy, but at the threat of what they promised.

Ceff and I had been dating for a few months now, but we hadn't actually touched yet. No hand holding or stolen kisses in the dark. I had already experienced traumatic visions from handling a piece of Ceff's bridle and wasn't quite ready to risk touching the man himself. Coming into physical contact with something old always increased the risk of multiple visions, and Ceff was ancient. What would it be like to kiss an immortal kelpie king?

I wasn't ready to find out, yet.

I dug in my pocket, covering my retreat by checking my phone. No new messages. That in itself was a Christmas miracle.

Ever since I agreed to take Forneus' first case, and helped to protect the city against invading, bloodthirsty *each uisge*, our phones had been ringing off the hook. Jinx had cases scheduled for every day of the week going into the New Year. Business at Private Eye investigations was booming.

Apparently the fae who lived in Harborsmouth were in need of a private investigator. Jinx and I were happy to fill that niche. But working with fae meant calls at all hours, and Jinx could only field so many of our clients.

More often than not, the job was something that couldn't wait. When someone with fangs and claws shows up and says it's urgent, you know it's a real emergency. Your options are to either drop everything or turn tail and run. I really picked the wrong time for a social life.

I guess I should give Ceff a break. I'd had to cancel my share of dates due to emergency cases.

But now here we were, Ceff and I alone with no beasties breathing down my neck for the services of Ivy Granger psychic detective and Ceff had to leave.

Story of my life.

*****

Jinx rolled her eyes at me while I went back to sipping my noxious coffee. I was at Jinx's mercy when it came to the grocery shopping, since touching shopping carts and bags of coffee beans was always a bad idea, so I tried to keep her in a good mood. Maybe I could convince her to buy some real coffee. The kind that didn't taste like it was brewed with cookies, or someone's old fruit cake.

"Sorry, you're right," I said. "Ceff didn't really want to go. I'm just frustrated."

"Of course you're frustrated," Jinx said. She put a hand on one voluptuous hip and pointed a well manicured finger at me. "You're a twenty-four year old virgin."

"Well...well, I have a unicorn!" I said.

I crossed my arms wishing Jinx would butt out of my non-existent sex life. I'd hoped that she'd back off once I started dating. Instead, my relationship with Ceff just seemed to fuel her need to interfere.

Jinx turned and wiped her eyes with a dish towel. Was she crying? I was grumpy, but Jinx was used to my mood swings, especially before my first cup of coffee. She set down the towel, looked at me, and started laughing.

"Oh my God, you should see yourself right now," she said.

"What?" I asked.

"Dude, you sound like you're five," she said. "And you're dressed in little kid pajamas."

"You bought me these pajamas," I said.

"I know," she said, sniffing and dabbing at her makeup.

"You suck," I said.

"Yes," she said.

"And this coffee tastes like stale cookies," I said.

"Totally," she said, nodding. "It was a Christmas gift from Olly. He has a skateboard competition in Oakland, so he dropped it off last night before leaving town."

"He bought us coffee?" I asked.

"He probably regifted it," she said, shrugging one tattooed shoulder.

"That makes more sense," I said. "And he's too much of a conspiracy buff to drink something someone else gave him. At least it wasn't Kool-Aid. He would have freaked."

"Plus, one whiff and he'd know it smelled like gingerbread men died in there," she said. "It's no wonder he gave the whole bag away."

"Seriously," I said. "Nastiest coffee ever."

"Want another cup?" she asked.

"Sure," I said.

It tasted gross, but a girl needs her caffeine fix. I gulped it down while Jinx took another dainty sip.

"You know what?" Jinx asked. "This probably tastes exactly like cookie monster pee."

I spit gingerbread coffee all over the counter. Jinx could be a total pain, but she really has a way with words.

And the two of us living together?—always entertaining.

CHAPTER 2

I was finishing up with my morning client when I heard a commotion at the front of the office. Greeting clients was Jinx's job, but with the variety of faeries seeking our services lately, I figured I'd better check things out.

There aren't any walls between my desk and Jinx's, or the front door, but the mother bugbear sitting in front of me was doing a fine impersonation. Adult bugbears are not only huge, but they're also covered in fur. This one's auburn fur stuck out in every direction, making it impossible to see what was happening at the front of the room.

I stood, on the pretense of fetching a glass of water, and peered around the bulk of my oversized client.

Damn. Forneus was standing in our office doorway and Jinx was brandishing a sharpened cross like she was a rockabilly incarnation of Buffy the vampire slayer. As I watched in horror, Jinx lifted the edge of her dress and slid a second cross from a sheath on her thigh. My office assistant got bonus points for style and preparedness, but I really didn't think killing our clients was good for business—especially with a bugbear sitting, oblivious, at my desk. Any second now my satisfied client was going to turn around and reconsider the agency she hired, and our payment.

No way was I losing that fee. Tracking down that cub took me over a week. And bugbear wrangling is no treat. I worked hard for every penny and I wasn't letting Jinx and Forneus' flirtatious fighting scare off my client.

Plus, I needed that money to pay for coffee. There was no way I was beginning another day drinking the stuff Olly gifted us. Not after Jinx's comment. I'd picture a fuzzy, blue monster singing "C is for coffee" while peeing into my cup.

That settled it. I needed to take control of the situation, quickly.

"Let me just get the invoice from my assistant and we'll be done here," I said, smiling at the bugbear.

I tried not to show my teeth. Flash too much tooth and some predators will think you are issuing a challenge. I did not need to add a bugbear pissing contest to an already bad situation. I don't think our office would survive that level of chaos. I know that I'm not up for that fight. Have you seen the size of their claws?

I walked casually past the bugbear who was eyeing my dish of honey candies. I discovered while hanging out with my friends Marvin and Hob, a bridge troll and a brownie, that pureblood fae have a weakness for sweets, especially honey. I kept the dish of candies on hand for situations like these.

Now that my clientele has changed, I may not be able to keep the office warded and filled with anti-fae charms, but I still kept a few tricks up my sleeve. It never hurt to be prepared.

"What do you two think you're doing?" I hissed. I turned my full wrath on Jinx. She didn't even flinch. Guess I can't be scary when a person's seen me in my snowman pajamas. "What happened?"

"That damn demon is here again," Jinx said, never taking her eyes off Forneus. "That's what happened."

"That's all?" I asked. "He came through the door and you tried to stake him with a cross?"

"I can assure you that I have done nothing untoward," Forneus said. His sulphuric breath made me gag. "I merely offered this lovely lady a compliment."

"What did he call you this time?" I asked.

"He called me his pet," she said through clenched teeth. "I warned him last time that if he addressed me that way again, I'd kill him."

"She did warn you," I said, turning to the demon. I took a step forward to stand between them. "But, as much as I'd like to see her cut you with that cross, I have a client waiting— a *paying* client."

That last bit of info was for Jinx. She immediately lowered her weapons and slid them neatly into her hair and up the skirt of her halter dress.

"I'll get the paperwork," Jinx said. She hurried to her desk and pointed at the chairs arranged beside it. "You take a seat, demon. And don't even think about leaving one of your business cards in my waiting room."

"Yes, ma'am," he said.

The demon folded himself primly into one of our mismatched chairs—mismatched because we had to douse a chair with holy water and trash it after one of Forneus' earlier visits. Just for the record, burning brimstone is Hell on upholstery. He was lucky we let him walk through our doors at all.

I walked back to mother bugbear, who was miraculously still sitting facing my desk. A glance at my empty candy dish showed why. I'd have to restock my supply soon.

I saw a trip to the candy store in my future.

I may not like to shop, but going to the candy store with Marvin was a treat. I didn't have to touch anything, since the kid was happy to put everything in the basket for me. With no worries about psychic visions, I could kick back and watch Marvin's smile grow.

Marvin's smile was worth the effort. His mouth was healing from his previous injuries and the kid was looking better by the day. Not that anyone in the candy shop could see his true face. Marvin was one of the fae, a teenage bridge troll, and wore his glamour whenever we hit the streets.

I'd check in with Marvin later. I had an errand to run at Madam Kaye's Magic Emporium, and Hob was still allowing Marvin to sleep on the floor of the spell kitchen, out behind the shop. The place may be owned by Kaye O'Shaye, the most powerful witch in Harborsmouth, but Hob, the resident hearth brownie, was in charge of the kitchen. I could visit Marvin, get the items I needed from The Emporium, and be back before dark...if Forneus didn't hold me up.

"Here you are," Jinx said, setting a folder on my desk. Jinx beamed at the bugbear as she pointed to the folder. "Just read and sign the last page. And make checks payable to Private Eye. We're also happy to accept cash and all major credit cards."

The mother bugbear lifted a leather pouch onto the desk with a thud. Gold coins spilled from the bag as she scratched her mark onto the page, with her claws.

"Ivy?" Jinx asked.

I knew what Jinx was asking. In addition to psychometry, I also have the gift of second sight. My second sight allows me to see through the glamour that most fae wear to the monstrous visage that lies beneath. This was another gift that could feel like a curse, but it was a talent that came in handy when accepting payment from faeries.

Fae, both Seelie and Unseelie, have an aversion to paying humans real money. Since humans usually can't see through magical glamour, faeries often pay with illusionary money that reverts to its original worthless form after they have safely gone. It wouldn't be the first time that a faerie tried to pay with leaves and twigs. But this gold was real.

And I wasn't human.

I nodded to Jinx.

"We also accept gold," Jinx said, smiling.

Jinx led the bugbear out the door and I strode over to where Forneus sat in his expensive suit. I crossed my arms and tapped my foot.

"Okay, demon, why are you here?" I asked.

Forneus spread his hands and opened his eyes wide in mock surprise.

"Can't a friend drop in without a reason?" he asked. "'Tis the season after all. Perhaps I'm here to spread holiday cheer."

"Or an STD," Jinx muttered.

Jinx closed the door behind our bugbear client and came to sit on the edge of her desk. She sucked air through her teeth and winced. The reason became clear when she pulled a thumb tack from her generous derriere. Jinx really was the most unlucky person on the planet. Which made taunting a demon a ridiculously bad idea.

"I will have you know that..." Forneus said.

"No," I said, holding up a gloved hand. "No way. I do not want to hear about your sexual exploits. I don't care where your pitchfork has been, Forneus, just keep it in your pants."

"Amen," Jinx said.

Forneus grimaced at the holy word, but continued to leer at Jinx. She was adjusting the bust of her fifties-style halter dress in a not so subtle attempt to drive Forneus crazy. Watching the demon lust over my best friend made my stomach heave. It was time to change the subject.

"So what's the job?" I asked, rubbing my brow. Forneus had only been here a few minutes and already I had a headache. "And don't tell me that this is just a social call."

"Well, I do have information you may find valuable," Forneus said. "For a price."

Forneus' eyes glowed red and his face shifted as the muscles writhed beneath the skin. It was a reminder that our guest wasn't human. Forneus may wear a handsome face while doing business, but his preferred form while topside was a leviathan-like beast the size of our entire city block. I didn't know what form the demon attorney took when residing in Hell, but the glowing red eyes were a clue.

I stifled a shudder and met those eyes determined not to let Forneus get the upper hand.

"No deals with the devil, Forneus," I said. "If your information is useful, we can work something out, but no souls, or dates with my partner, as payment. And if what you have to say isn't of use to us, then we owe you nothing."

Forneus steepled his fingers and frowned, deep in thought. After three minutes, I was beginning to wonder if he'd fallen asleep. Do demons sleep? I'd have to ask Father Michael the next time I went to visit Galliel at St. Mary's church.

"If this becomes a significant case, I want full credit for bringing this information to you," he said.

Demons were always fighting to advance within their social hierarchy and Forneus was no different. He had received a promotion for his role in bringing me the kelpie case, and the resulting battle that case had caused. Now I couldn't get rid of the ambitious fiend.

"Deal," I said.

The demon reached a hand out to shake on our agreement, and I danced out of reach.

"You know the rules," I said, voice hardening.

"Ah, yes," he said, leaning back in his chair. "No touching."

"So we have a deal?" I asked.

"Deal," he said.

A grin spread over his face and I began to doubt my decision to agree so quickly.

"What did you find out?" I asked.

"Someone is killing fae, right here in Harborsmouth," he said.

I really was going to regret this. Forneus wasn't bringing me a typical lost and found case, he was talking about murder.

"How many dead?" I asked.

"Five that I know of, all fae," he said. "And before you ask, they are not all Seelie or Unseelie. Both courts have received victims."

Oh, Oberon's eyes. If the victims had all been from one court, then I'd know where to begin looking for their killer. But this wasn't an overzealous faerie trying to curry favor with their Lord by assassinating members of the opposing court. This was something else entirely.

There was a serial killer in Harborsmouth with a penchant for murdering faeries. Happy freaking holidays.

CHAPTER 3

According to Forneus, five fae had been murdered on the streets of Harborsmouth. But what did a peri, a hamadryad, a merry dancer, a pixie, and old Fear Dearg have in common?

The only clue to tie these deaths together was a piece of mistletoe left at each scene. Well, that and the fact that shortly after each victim was discovered, their body disappeared.

Since mistletoe was our one clue, Christmas was the obvious connection. Maybe someone had a thing against Santa's elves and was killing the next best thing.

I shook my head. No, that was just silly. Santa didn't exist and the elves had left our shores long ago.

But why kill these particular fae?

I stared at the list I'd hastily penciled onto a notepad, trying to make sense of these murders. If I couldn't ferret out the truth on my own, I'd have to ask Kaye for help. And if I couldn't find answers at The Emporium, I'd have to visit each of the crime scenes. Touching a person's wedding ring to see if they've been cheating on their spouse is one thing, but handling items at a murder scene is quite another. I shuddered and returned my focus to the notepad on my desk.

Peris are small, winged men often mistaken for angels. Their diminutive size makes them vulnerable to their natural enemy, the daeva, who enjoy locking them in iron cages at the tops of trees. Had our killer wanted a sick tree topper for his Christmas tree?

I shook my head, trying to shake away the image. I was just letting the holidays, and my own dark mood, get to me, right? Maybe the other victims would reveal a pattern.

A hamadryad was the second faerie on the list. Hamadryads are tree nymphs who are peaceful unless their tree is threatened. Hamadryads are very protective of their chosen tree and have been known to keep a tree alive for hundreds of years. But if a hamadryad dies, the tree they are bound to dies with it. Forneus indicated that this hamadryad had come from a fir tree, which was peculiar for a city dryad. There aren't many trees in Harborsmouth and even fewer evergreens. I wonder which city park or old tree lined street was mourning the loss of its fir tree. Or had the killer cut it down as a gruesome souvenir?

This case was beginning to leave a bad taste in my mouth worse than this morning's coffee.

I didn't know a lot about my cousins the merry dancers. While researching my wisp heritage, I'd found mention of them, but most sources just referenced the beautiful, colorful lights they produced when they danced through the air. Do merry dancers continue to glow after death? Had the merry dancer been killed to light the hamadryad's tree?

I glared at the list of victims, gripping my pencil so hard the edges bit through my thick gloves. A tree, an angel, and lights? Mab's bloody bones, holidays were Hell.

I wasn't surprised to see a pixie on the list of victims. Even I'd been tempted to kill a few of the pests over the years. Pixies are the fae equivalent of wasps. They may have beautiful, iridescent wings, but don't let that fool you. The evil little creatures are armed with a stinger the size of a hypodermic needle. One sting will paralyze a grown human, but pixies are rarely solitary. As soon as one of the bastards has you down, the entire hive is likely to use your body as a salt lick. Pixies survive on salt, too bad their saliva is an allergen that itches like the devil. Take it from me; being pixed sucks.

Was the pixie now hanging as a bloody ornament on the killer's tree, iridescent wings reflecting a rainbow of color in the glow of the merry dancer's light? The thought made bile rise in my throat. I may not like the little insects, but no one deserved to be strung on a tree. Not even a pixie.

Fear Dearg was the one faerie on the list whom I had met. I had made the mistake of running errands during the holidays last year and got turned around. As the maze-like store became more crowded, a band of iron tightened around my chest. I needed to escape the press of shoppers before I hyperventilated and passed out. I did not want to be one of those holiday victims trampled to death by their fellow shoppers.

I was ready to vault onto a display case and take my chances running along the tops of shopping carts and clothing racks when Fear Dearg had appeared. Dressed in a red coat and hat and long white beard, he looked like a stand-in for old Saint Nick. He had pointed to the exit, put a finger to his nose, and vanished. When I mentioned the encounter later, Kaye told me that Fear Dearg had once been a benevolent faerie who helped lost travelers on the moors. But the moors and peat bogs had been drained. Now Fear Dearg helped Allmart shoppers find their way to the housewares department, and lead panicky psychics to the exit. The modern world hadn't been kind to some of the fae. And now someone had killed the poor man.

"Are we really taking this case?" Jinx asked.

I thought about old Fear Dearg's rosy cheeked smile as he helped me find my way out of that store filled with holiday shoppers.

"Yes," I said. "I think this sicko is killing fae to create some kind of twisted Christmas diorama."

Jinx wrinkled her nose.

"Sounds like a total nut job," Jinx said. "Leave it to the holidays to bring out the crazies."

Jinx was right. The holidays are dangerous enough when the people going insane are human. Add faeries, demons, and the undead to the mix and you get a recipe for something truly nasty. Now we just had to figure out who was doing the killing.

And who was stealing the bodies.

I swallowed hard and reached for the cup of water I'd left sitting beside the dish of honey candies. We had our water cooler blessed by a local priest, but the holy water didn't taste any different than regular spring water. Holy water doesn't have any effect on faeries, but throw it on a demon and you had a weapon more corrosive than hydrochloric acid. Too bad we weren't dealing with a demon. That much seemed obvious.

A demon wouldn't have left sprigs of mistletoe floating in a pool of blood. Demons reap souls, preferring to play with their prey in Hell where they are at their most powerful. If our killer was a demon, he'd have left only a charred, soulless husk behind.

"I don't think our nut job is a demon," I said.

Jinx snorted. "Why not?" she asked.

Jinx rested her hand on her skirt where I'd seen one of her sharpened crosses disappear. I was glad we weren't looking for Hellspawn. I'd never keep Jinx safely in the office if we were gunning for a demon. Forneus had a habit of getting under her skin and today's visit hadn't helped her aversion toward demons.

"Nothing was burned at the scene," I said, tapping the notepad. "No charred remains."

"Okay, gag, that's nasty," she said. "But shouldn't we check the crime scenes ourselves? I don't trust Forneus. It would be just like that creep to leave out an important detail like faeries fried extra crispy or a lingering cloud of sulphur and brimstone."

Sadly, Jinx was right. I couldn't trust Forneus. I'd have to see the crime scenes for myself.

"I'll check the scenes later," I said. "But first I need to ask Kaye about the victims. She has more knowledge of the supernatural races than anyone else in the city. If there's a connection I'm missing, she'll know."

"Ask her to check with her Hunter friends too," she said. "Maybe they've heard something about the murders. And, of course, if they want to lend one of their big, strong, Hunters to come protect our offices, I won't complain."

Jinx batted her eyelashes and tried to look helpless. I knew better. She may look like a rockabilly damsel in distress, but Jinx could flay a person's soul with a good tongue lashing. She could give a drill sergeant a run for his money. I should know. She spent most of her time keeping me in line.

"I'd ask, but they'd probably send Jenna," I said.

Jenna was a young, female Hunter I'd met during the *each uisge* invasion of Harborsmouth. Jenna is petite, wears her flame red hair in a short, cute, pixie cut, and is always armed to the teeth. When we first met she wore a sword at her hip, knives in a forearm sheath, a gun holster strapped around her thigh, and held a crossbow trained at my head. I have that effect on people.

"I need some eye candy," Jinx said waggling her eyebrows. "Tell them to send Hans."

Hans was a tall, Nordic drink of water who looked like a Norse God. Fought like one too. The guy was gorgeous enough to give Jinx a toothache, but Hans was also known for his berserker-like rages. Angry rampaging on the battlefield was usually beneficial, especially when the desired outcome was a high body count, but it wasn't a quality I wanted in someone dating my best friend. Leave it to Jinx to always pick the bad boys.

"Sure, I'll do that," I said, rolling my eyes. "While I'm at it, I'll ask a leprechaun for his pot of gold. I have about the same chances of him saying yes."

The Hunter's Guild didn't owe me any favors. In fact, their assistance in the recent battle against the *each uisge* army had helped to save my city. I knew that the Hunters hadn't fought for me, they were there to back up Kaye, a former hunter, and to defend the humans of Harborsmouth, but it felt like I owed them. Of course, if they ever wanted to collect on that debt, they'd have to get in line.

"Then bring me back a coffee," she said, pouting. "That demon gave me a headache."

"That, I can do," I said.

I pulled on my coat, tucking the notepad in one pocket and a fistful of charms into another. Being half-fae had its perks. Most anti-fae charms, such as rowanberry, stale bread, clothing turned inside out, four-leafed clovers, and cold iron, didn't affect me.

We may have put away most of our protection items in consideration for our new clientele, but that didn't mean I went around unarmed. I kept a stash of iron nails, sharpened stakes, holy water, and silver crosses in my desk drawer. I was an equal opportunity kind of girl—you never know what might slink, slither, crawl, fly, or dance through your door. It was best to be prepared for the worst.

If a faerie, a vampire, and a demon walk into a bar, you wait for the punch line. At Private Eye, when a faerie, a vampire, and a demon walk through the door, it's just another day at the office.

CHAPTER 4

If it wasn't for the holidays, winter would be my favorite season. A cold, arctic wind blew across the harbor to tug at my scarf and bite my nose. I pulled my coat tighter and smiled.

Winter is the one time of year when I feel normal. I can walk the streets of Harborsmouth without strange looks, curious stares, and stolen glances. Wearing gloves when it's freezing cold outside is completely reasonable, but wear those same gloves in the melting heat of summer and passerby are likely to think you belong locked away with Aunt Edna's fruitcake.

I ignored the wreath and garland bedecked lamp posts as I made my way through the Old Port toward Kaye's shop. Holiday decorations?—bah humbug. I'd rather the city invest its money in putting sand on our sidewalks.

I trudged through the slush along the curb, avoiding the ice slick walkways. The sidewalks in this part of town were made of dark red brick that matched the old buildings that lined the street. During the day, water dripped down from icicles the size of yeti fangs to threaten those who walked beneath and dampen the ice below. At night the puddles froze, turning this brick sidewalk into a narrow skating rink...at a forty-five degree pitch. More than one drunk had stumbled out the door of an Old Port bar and ended up in the harbor.

I'd take my chances with the cobblestone street.

I turned up Wharf Street where Madame Kaye's Magic Emporium perched at the top of the hill like a queen in a purple and midnight blue gown trimmed with gold. Astrological symbols covered the wood and brick façade while overflowing cauldrons, tarot decks, Halloween costumes, and packets of herbs fought for space in the shop windows.

I hurried my pace, the wind now at my back, and pushed open the door. Wind chimes sang and the plastic bones of skeletons rattled as a rush of cold air made its way into the store.

"Close the door, dear, before my face freezes this way," Kaye said.

I pushed the door closed and turned to see Kaye glaring at her assistant Arachne with one eye scrunched up tight. Arachne was facing Kaye and mirroring the expression.

"Um, am I interrupting something?" I asked.

Kaye was the most powerful witch in all of Harborsmouth, possibly the entire eastern seaboard. If she was angry, I wanted to be somewhere else, fast.

"Hey, Ivy," Arachne said. She smiled and waved, the angry expression leaving her face. "Kaye was teaching me the Evil Eye. Cool, huh?"

Arachne worked part time at The Emporium in hopes of becoming Kaye's apprentice. Arachne was sixteen, blond, and a hard worker. She was also completely gullible.

Kaye likes to play tricks on her human employees, which is why they usually don't last long. Arachne had been here the longest, but Kaye never tired of pranking her. If I didn't know better, I'd say Kaye had a puck in her bloodline.

I looked over at Kaye, who was pulling faces behind Arachne's back, and groaned.

"Are you going to tell her, or should I?" I asked.

Kaye started laughing, the bells on her bracelets and anklets jiggling, and waved for me to go on. I turned back to Arachne and her face fell.

"Oh, it wasn't a real lesson, was it?" she asked.

"Sorry, kid," I said.

Kaye let out a snort and dabbed at her kohl rimmed eyes with the corner of her head scarf.

"Don't worry, dear," Kaye said. "I'll teach you a truth spell later. It will be worth more to you than an Evil Eye."

It was true that Arachne could use a truth spell working here, but knowing Kaye she'd know a way around her own spell. It wouldn't do to spoil her fun and trickery.

Arachne nodded and moved behind the counter where she started counting and tagging packets of incense. Kaye hustled toward the rear of the store and I followed. The jumble of wares that cluttered the aisles closed around us as we made our way to the back of the store where a secret button let us past the counter, through a beaded curtain, and into a hallway that led to Kaye's small office on one side and her spell kitchen on the other.

Kaye turned left and I followed her into the kitchen where Marvin sat on the floor. Hob was flitting around Marvin's head, attaching something to his face.

"Hello, Hob," I said. I acknowledged Hob first, since brownies were particular about such things, and easily angered. Orphaned bridge trolls, on the other hand, were much more forgiving. "Hello, Marvin."

"Hello, Poison Ivy," Marvin said, grinning.

The kid never got tired of that one. Hob fussed as the gray stuff he was attaching to Marvin's face shifted with the wide grin. Hob harrumphed and stomped a booted foot on Marvin's shoulder.

"Told ye ta sit still," Hob said.

"Why don't you both take a break," Kaye said.

I thought Hob would complain, but instead he flew toward me so fast I stumbled over my own two feet. He stopped, perching on a pot hook above my head. There was a greedy gleam in the eyes that peeked from below his large, bushy brow.

"Where be me gift?" Hob asked.

I may have a fear of handling strange gifts, but Hob had no such compunction. I had entered the hearth brownie's domain and he expected his payment. It was tradition and faeries take such things very seriously indeed.

I dipped my gloved hand into the pocket of my coat and pulled out a small pigeon feather wrapped in shiny tissue paper. I always kept small gifts with me in case I visited Kaye's kitchen. I'd rather stumble into a nest of pixies than enter Hob's domain without bringing his payment. There is nothing worse than an angry brownie.

I set the present on the nearby counter and stepped away. Hob circled the tiny package, dancing a jig on the white tiled countertop. Even if he didn't care for the dove gray feather, I figured he'd like the tissue paper. Brownies adore shiny things.

Hob pounced on the package, stripping the tissue from the feather. He examined the feather so closely it tickled his bulbous red nose. His nose twitched, but Hob continued to hold the feather to his face.

"Is the gift acceptable?" I asked.

As much as I enjoyed visiting with Hob and Marvin, I really did have questions for Kaye. My father's blood may add extra years to my lifespan, but I couldn't wait around here forever. Whoever was killing faeries in our city had to be stopped.

"Aye, lass," Hob said.

I let out the breath I'd been holding and moved further into the kitchen.

"So what's with the get up?" I asked, nodding at Marvin.

"Play," Marvin said.

Were the troll and brownie playing dress up? That was new.

"We are putting on a theatrical performance," Kaye said. "During the solstice party."

"Aye, the Changling Child," Hob said. He put a knobby finger to the side of his nose.

"I don't think I've seen that one," I said. "What part are you playing, Marvin?"

"Wise man," he said.

Now that I thought about it, the cloth covering Marvin's head and shoulders did resemble a hooded cloak. The gray stuff Hob had been attaching to Marvin's face must have been a beard.

"And you, Hob?" I asked.

"Ta changling babe!" he said, slapping his knee. Hob laughed and wiped his eyes with the back of his sleeve. "Dis wise man bring me gold."

I had a sinking feeling about what holiday story they were doing a faerie retelling of. The image of the shriveled old brownie swaddled in a manger made me cringe. Changeling tales had always given me the creeps.

Faeries rarely have children of their own and have been known to steal human infants. The human child is whisked away and an elderly faerie left in its place. The unsuspecting humans will often take care of the invalid fae while their baby is raised by faeries. Unfortunately, faerie child rearing often includes slave-like servitude. I hid my shudder with a shrug.

"Cool, can't wait to see the show," I said. "So, Kaye, I had an interesting visitor today."

"Was it that demon?" she asked.

"Yes," I said, tilting my head to the side. "How did you know?"

"I strengthened my wards," she said. Kaye had been upset when Forneus first entered the city without her knowledge. Apparently, she'd been working to remedy that problem. "An alarm sounds when a demon enters the city, but he was gone before I had a chance to investigate."

"Is that the only demon you've sensed entering Harborsmouth recently?" I asked.

"Yes, no other demon would be so foolish," she said.

That confirmed my original suspicion. Our killer wasn't a demon. We were looking for a faerie, an undead, or…a human.

I filled Kaye, Marvin, and Hob in on the details of the case. Kaye stomped across the floor, jewelry jingling and skirts rustling as she paced back and forth. She may be a retired Hunter, but Kaye was a fierce protector of this city. Knowing that someone had managed to kill five fae under her nose had upset her.

Marvin chewed his lip and stared at the floor.

Hearing about faerie murders had to be hard on the kid. A bridge troll probably doesn't sound like an easy target for a beating, but Marvin was a teenager and an orphan. He had been struggling to live alone on the streets when the *each uisge* came to Harborsmouth. When the bloodthirsty water fae attacked, the kid never stood a chance. If the *each uisge* hadn't had more interesting prey that night, Marvin would be dead. His wounds were healing, but the emotional scars were going to take a while longer.

Good thing I knew a way to cheer the kid up.

"Hey, Marvin," I said. "My bugbear client ate all of the honey candies in my office. Want to take a trip to the candy store later?"

Marvin nodded and smiled.

"How about you take off your costume, dear, while I speak to Ivy in my office," Kaye said.

Kaye bustled out into the hallway and I hurried to catch up.

"I'll be back in an hour, Marvin," I said, following Kaye to the door. "Hour and a half tops. I have a few items to stock up on from the shop and then I'll come meet you here." I waved to both Marvin and Hob. "Safe travels."

"Safe travels, lass," Hob said.

I entered Kaye's office to a cloud of dust that made my eyes water. I pinched my nose, stifling a sneeze, and watched as Kaye used her magic to move books and documents around the room. Books covered every surface of Kaye's office and formed precarious towers that reached to the ceiling. With a twitch of Kaye's finger and a twist of her wrist, leather bound tomes and yellowed papers slid out of the leaning towers and whizzed past her face. If it wasn't for Kaye's magic, we'd be buried in a book avalanche.

"Here it is," Kaye said, holding an object triumphantly over her head.

I moved closer, ducking as a sheaf of papers flew past my nose. I stepped back, not wanting anything of Kaye's to touch my bare skin. Kaye may be my friend, but her arcane collection of spell tomes, ritual items, and occult books has been passed down from one magic user to the next—steeped in centuries of blood and madness.

The papers rustled as they rushed forward and slid beneath one of the book towers to my left. I held my breath as a crystal ball, which had been sitting atop the stack of books, teetered back and forth. If the scrying crystal tipped over the edge, I knew one private investigator who wouldn't be catching it.

Kaye reached up to smooth her wild raven locks, and I let out a sigh of relief as the items settled back into place. She waved me forward and I tiptoed through piles of magical detritus as if compelled. But this time Kaye wasn't using her magic. My boots were finding their way across the office because of the item in Kaye's hand. Her heavily beringed fingers held a well worn volume from a set of herbal encyclopedias.

Of course, Kaye's compendium of herbs went beyond what plants to grow in your garden. These books contained the magical uses, both good and wicked, for each herb—seed, stem, leaf, and root. I had perused a few of these volumes when researching protection charms. Some of the entries were fairly benign, but others had left my stomach in knots and had given me nightmares for a week. Since I already had my share of nightmares, I hoped the information on mistletoe fell into the safe and boring category.

No such luck.

"Here," Kaye said.

With another puff of dust, Kaye dropped the open book onto her desk and tapped the page with one tattooed finger. The black swirls of ink hadn't reached her hands before the *each uisge* attack. I winced and made a mental note to ask her about it later. It seemed like lately all I had for my friend was questions.

I leaned forward to see what Kaye was pointing at. The old etching depicted a man reaching for his throat. His eyes were bulging and his tongue was black.

Mistletoe was poisonous. It was also used during the holidays as an excuse to sneak a kiss. I wasn't sure which was worse.

According to the book, mistletoe was poisonous when the leaves or berries were ingested. It was also considered dangerous to inhale the smoke. For these reasons, mistletoe was not used in magical teas, tisanes, incense, and ritual fires. However the plant did have many magical uses.

Mistletoe was used by the Druids to alter states of consciousness and induce visions. The plant was also commonly used in ritual sacrifice. I swallowed hard and skimmed past the diagrams depicting the stomach contents of sacrificial victims.

My leather glove creaked like a coffin lid as I rubbed at the back of my stooped neck. Could our killer be reenacting some form of ritualistic murder? I sure hope not. Reading one encyclopedic entry on sacrifice was enough nightmare fodder for an entire lifetime.

In the cases of sacrifice involving mistletoe, the victims were force fed the plant then subjected to a three-fold death. The first death was caused by blows to the head with a blunt instrument. The second death involved strangulation, hanging, or breaking of the neck. The third death was secured with a blade to the victim's carotid artery. Got to love that human sacrifice.

"This three-fold death thing is disgusting," I said.

I pointed to the sketch of a victim succumbing to each stage of death. The drawing was worse than the diagram of stomach contents.

"The number three is significant to humans and the fae," Kaye said, shrugging. "At least the victims ate or imbibed the mistletoe first. That was a kindness. The sacrificial lamb would hallucinate and die from poison before realizing the horrors of the first beating."

Kaye seemed unfazed by the stories of sacrifice. Had she taken part in such a ritual in her past? I shook my head.

No way. My friend may have a practical approach to magic and its uses, but she wouldn't step over that line. Kaye had given her life to protecting humans. She wouldn't go around using them as spell components.

"So mistletoe is a poison and a part of murderous rituals," I said. "What else?"

I had a feeling that Kaye knew most of the wisdom found in her library.

"Mistletoe is a magical amplifier," Kaye said. "Adding the plant or berries to almost any magic, good or evil, will increase the desired outcome of a spell. The mistletoe that grows on oak trees is the most powerful, but any type will do."

"Great, this stuff acts like a shot of energy drink to casters," I said. "Is that it?"

"Just a question, dear," she said. "Was there anything else at the scene? Perhaps something that could indicate what magic, if any, was being used."

I thought back to my conversation with Forneus. According to the demon, the only thing left at the crime scenes, once the bodies disappear, was mistletoe and blood. I ran a gloved hand through my hair and voiced the idea that came unbidden to my lips.

"Blood," I said. "At every scene there was blood. I assumed it was from the act of murder itself. But..."

"It could be something else entirely," she said, nodding. "Blood magic is powerful, hostile. Mistletoe may amplify the outcome of a spell, but blood amplifies both the magic and the emotions of the caster."

"Let me guess," I said, giving Kaye a mirthless smile. "That doesn't usually end well."

"No, it never does," Kaye said. "Blood magic ends badly, indeed."

"Could someone be using this kind of magic in Harborsmouth without you knowing?" I asked, staring at the books that lined the walls.

I couldn't meet Kaye's eyes. She worked hard to spread her awareness over our city, like a magical security blanket to protect innocent humans from harm. But like any hand knit afghan, Kaye's awareness spell had holes. She had tightened the magical threads that detected demons, but that didn't mean something else couldn't slip through.

I darted my gaze in time to see my friend's shoulders slump. Kaye's head dipped to her chest as she let out a sigh. Kaye was a tough old bird. That sigh said it all.

"I'm not getting any younger, dear," Kaye said. She lifted her head to meet my eyes, but a bleak look had replaced the fire I was used to seeing reflected in their black depths. Kaye raised a hand, wiggling her fingers. The bell sleeves of her blouse fell back to reveal a mass of twining tattoos. "My magic comes at a price. I do what I can, but yes, someone could be practicing blood magic without my knowing."

Since the *each uisge* attack, I'd been lucky. Business was booming and Jinx and I had settled into our daily routine. I was courting an immortal kelpie king, and my witch friend, with the aid of every magic user in the region, had cast a spell more powerful than anything I'd ever seen. For the first time since becoming aware of the monsters that walked our streets, I had felt safe.

I was a fool.

Now I was taking another job from a demon, Ceffyl was away negotiating water fae treaties, someone was killing faeries like they were mosquitoes, and my all-powerful witch friend was admitting that she wasn't all-powerful after all. I ducked my head, feeling vulnerable. I felt like someone had attached a bull's eye to my back—right next to the "kick me" sign and "world's biggest idiot" post-it note. For most people, letting their guard down is a healthy thing. In Harborsmouth, it will just get you dead.

"Okay, what can I do?" I asked.

"Visit the murder scenes and see what else you can find," she said. "The sooner we know what we're dealing with, the better. And Ivy? Don't forget your plan to stock up on protection herbs and amulets. I'll call the front desk and inform Arachne that you aren't to be charged for today's purchases."

"Um, thanks," I said.

"Yes, of course, dear," she said, waving me away. "Now go. After my call to Arachne, I will contact the Hunter's guild. They should be made aware of the threat to the city. Hunters may have vowed to protect humans against supernatural forces, but they won't take kindly to someone murdering fae without their permission."

"Are you sure a Hunter didn't make these kills?" I asked.

"There have been no sanctioned kills or banishments in over two weeks," she said. I raised an eyebrow and she sighed. "I may be retired from active duty, but I retain an honorary seat on the Hunter's council. They keep me apprised of guild activities within Harborsmouth. Now go."

Kaye pulled a phone from her multi-layered skirts, effectively ending our conversation. I hadn't known about Kaye's involvement with the Hunter's council. My gaze darted to the tattoos covering the hand holding the phone to her ear. In fact, there was a lot I didn't know about my friend. But now, as always, wasn't the time to ask.

I spun on my heel and left the room.

CHAPTER 5

The Emporium was nearly as cluttered as Kaye's office. The only place in the building that wasn't full of stuff preparing to topple over and smother me to death was Kaye's spell kitchen. That was because A) Hob would never tolerate a mess near his hearth and B) One speck of the wrong ingredient in Kaye's pot would spell KABOOM. The shop, however, belonged on an episode of Hoarders.

Plastic skeletons and foam reaper scythes battled for space alongside straw brooms, and faux spider webs. At least, I think the webs aren't real. I ducked lower, avoiding a basketball-sized spider with its plethora of beady eyes. That thing had to be fake, right? I sighed and shook web from my hair. You never can tell at The Emporium.

I dodged pointy hats, Styrofoam gargoyles, and overflowing cauldrons. Unlike the spell pots in Kaye's kitchen, these cauldrons were made of black plastic. Prettily labeled packets of herbs, mostly benign, spilled over the rim of each cauldron and onto tables and shelves.

I dipped the fingertips of one gloved hand gingerly into a nearby pot and withdrew small packages of wolfsbane, hellebore, mandrake, and agrimony. Most of the herbs at Madame Kaye's Magic Emporium were mundane, not all. These plants, and the salt in my pocket, would provide some protection against black magic. The rowanberry, stale bread, nails, and iron shavings I'd brought from my office stash would be my backup against faeries.

I grabbed a handful of glitter-topped wooden pencils from where they protruded from a grinning skull. Those were for any vamps that got in my way. Who said stakes can't be pretty?

I carried the goods to the front counter where Arachne hunched over a box of rubber bats, pricing gun at the ready.

"Hey," I said, setting the items on the countertop. "Kaye said these were on the house. Do you still want to ring them up?"

"Thanks, Ivy," Arachne said. "Keeping inventory around here is like trying to count grains of sand in an hourglass. Just give me a sec."

"Sure thing," I said.

"Need a bag?" she asked after ringing up the goods. Arachne held up a paper bag with the store logo across the front.

"No thanks," I said.

I scooped up the herbs and dumped them into the inner pocket of my coat. I tucked the pencils into the back of my belt, careful to keep my shirt between the wood and my skin. Most of my visions came from touching items with my hands, but that didn't mean the rest of my hide was safe.

"You heading back to the kitchen?" she asked.

"Just long enough to tell Marvin I have to bail on our candy run," I said. I sighed, not looking forward to that conversation. "Later, Arachne."

"Safe travels," she said.

I shambled back to the rear of the store, not eager to disappoint Marvin. The bridge troll was one of the few people who I cared about in this town. Oh well, nothing I could do about it now. Kaye had pressed the issue of time, which meant I couldn't be wandering off to the candy store with Marvin. Not today.

I needed to visit the crime scenes and see if there was any evidence of blood magic. Maybe knock on doors and find out if there were any fae witnesses to the attacks. That kind of legwork might be safe enough if I was looking for a lost necklace or a runaway bugbear, but this time I was searching for a stone cold killer. There was no way I'd risk taking the kid with me.

It was the right decision, but that didn't stop the guilt that gnawed away at my insides. I pressed the button that unlocked the rear counter and pushed through the bead curtain into the hallway at the back. With a sigh, I knocked on the kitchen door and stepped inside.

I hoped that Hob wouldn't want another gift, this soon after my last visit, but if he required it, I'd give him one of the pencils in my belt. The pencils were as long as his stumpy legs, but at least they were shiny.

"Hi Hob," I said, looking around the kitchen. "Where's Marvin?"

Hob was dusting the large mantel that hung about the hearth. The wood shone, but Hob rubbed at the mantel like it was covered in grime.

"Up n' disappeared!" he said. Hob continued to rub at the wood, but moisture shone in his eyes. "I only ducked inta me hole for a second. I swear eet. But when I returned, da wee mite was gone."

A pile of cloth and fur sat on the floor, the costume Marvin had changed out of. The kid wouldn't just leave a mess like that on Hob's floor. He was smarter than that. My heart sank and a chill entered the hollow pit of my stomach. I stared at the discarded clothing and let the importance of Hob's words sink in. A serial killer who was targeting fae was out there somewhere and now Marvin was missing. My hands tightened into fists, making the leather of my gloves creak.

"Don't worry," I said. "I'll find him. But Hob? Make sure Kaye knows about this and have her call me the second anyone learns anything."

"Find 'im, lass," he said.

Hob didn't look away from his polishing as I spun on my heel and sprinted to the door. I ran out of the kitchen, through the shop, and onto the street. I needed to find those clues, and the killer, now more than ever.

CHAPTER 6

The old brick buildings pressed together like whispering neighbors, creating a narrow alley that resembled a badger hole, effectively blocking out the night sky. I strode forward and stopped beneath a rusty fire escape where Forneus claimed the merry dancer had met her demise. I rubbed the back of my neck and kicked at a piece of soiled newspaper. Not a pleasant place to die.

Wind whistled down the alley carrying the rotting tang of garbage and the copper scent of blood. What if Marvin lay crumpled in an alley like this? Was he alive, dead, or injured? The kid had been through so much already in his short life.

I jumped as a hand settled on my shoulder.

"You shouldn't let people sneak up on you," Jinx said.

I gasped and stepped away, letting my friend's hand drop to her side. Crap, Jinx had a point. Nobody should have been able to approach me unawares. Not only had Jinx, a human, entered the alley without my knowing, she'd gotten close enough to touch me. I shivered against the cold. My worry over Marvin was a potentially fatal distraction.

"And you shouldn't be here," I said with a shrug.

"Someone has to keep you on your toes," she said. "You sounded like a crazy person when you called the office. So I decided to close early and meet you here. I know how much the troll kid means to you."

"When I phoned to tell you I was coming here, it wasn't an invitation," I said. "Anyway, I'm working the case. If I find Marvin in the process, all the better."

"Face it," Jinx said. "You have a soft spot for strays."

"I do not," I said. I turned away from Jinx's knowing gaze and examined the ground at my feet. I had moved a nest of pookas into my old tree house and a family of gnomes into my parents' garden, but that had been necessary. Helping to relocate the homeless fae had been the practical thing to do, in both cases. "I just don't like seeing kids get hurt"

"Sure, you just keep telling yourself that," she said. Jinx moved closer, leaning forward to look over my shoulder. "You find anything?"

"Looks like blood," I said. I grabbed one of the pencils from my belt and scraped at the ground. A layer of red ice broke away from the dirty pavement and I swallowed hard. "Kaye thinks our killer may be using blood magic."

"Well that's not disturbing or anything," Jinx said, pointing at the red, ice covered slush. "You've successfully ruined frozen strawberry margaritas for me."

"I didn't ask you to be here," I said. I let out a sigh and stood. I turned in a circle, scanning the brick walls and shadowed doorways. "Come on. We might as well find out if anyone saw anything."

"That could be a waste of time, especially since humans can't see through glamour," she said. "Isn't there a faster way to get clues?"

I ran a gloved hand through my hair and let out a shaky sigh. My eyes cut to the frozen puddle of blood. Sure, there was a faster way, but it could also turn me into a raving lunatic. I usually put off touching the remains of dead things as a last resort.

I shoved my hands into my coat pockets and hunched against the wind. Something small and hard hit the tips of my gloved fingers, and with a crinkle of cellophane, I pulled the item from my pocket. A honey flavored candy sat on my gloved palm.

Damn. I wiped at my face with my sleeve as the chill air tried to freeze the tears that soaked my eyelashes. I should have been buying candy with Marvin. Instead, I was considering touching a frozen puddle of blood in a dirty alley, and Marvin was missing.

Happy freaking holidays.

"Yes, there is a faster way," I said, shuffling forward. "But I'll need your help."

"Sure, what do you need?" she asked.

I unwound my scarf and handed it to Jinx.

"If I start screaming, shove that in my mouth," I said. Her eyes widened, but Jinx nodded. "And if I don't stop screaming, pull me away from the blood...and wash it off my hands."

"Got it," she said.

Jinx forced a brave smile to her lips, but I could see the fear in her eyes. She knew what I wasn't saying. This method may be faster than pounding the pavement and rattling some cages, but it was much more dangerous. There was no guarantee that removing the blood would break the connection.

I looked down at the candy in my hand. The decision was a no brainer. If the vision got its hooks in me deep enough, I wouldn't be coming back. But if we didn't find Marvin soon, neither would he.

I knelt in the filthy slush of the alley, ignoring the ice cold water that seeped through my pants. It was time to find our killer, and bring Marvin home.

I took a deep breath and pulled my gloves off, one finger at a time. I felt naked and was glad for Jinx's steady presence at my back. If anyone had to see me like this, at least it was the one person I knew I could trust.

I stared at my bare hands and the frozen red liquid just inches away. What was about to come next wouldn't be pretty. Hopefully Jinx would keep me quiet enough to avoid any curious cops or passerby. If we were up on Joysen Hill, where vamps and other beasties routinely hunt, screams from a dark alley would be commonplace. Too bad we were on the edge of the Old Port. The last thing we needed was a tourist stumbling in and witnessing my bizarre investigation methods. I shook my head, banishing thoughts of screaming bystanders and police interrogations. I'd just have to put my faith in Jinx.

I plunged my right hand into the ice and gasped at the cold as it burned against my skin. I closed my eyes against the image of frozen blood touching my hand. Seconds later, the black of my eyelids was replaced with the image of a dying faerie. I had shifted from reality to a vision and the images were coming in full bloody Technicolor.

And the vision was coming from the perspective of the killer—oh goodie.

Warm liquid ran over my hands from the slashed neck of a merry dancer. I held a ceremonial knife to the faerie's throat and whispered guttural words in a foreign tongue. Scarlet threads of power rose from the body in radiant tendrils to twine up my legs and arms. I felt drunk on the rush of power as I drank the faerie's remaining life essence.

I staggered to my left, leaning against the brick wall of the alley. I steadied my hold on the faerie and the ritual blade in my blood slick hand. My eyes flicked down to the skeleton bundled in my cloak, resting in the shadows.

"Soon my beloved," I whispered.

I continued the incantation, careful to guide the stream of blood along the blade into the bottle nestled in the palm of my hand. The crystal bottle gleamed red and gold with an inner fire and thick black and scarlet smoke rose from within to swirl around the bottle's mouth. The magic was working.

Blood dripped into the bottle as I chanted, filling it to the brim. With a satisfied grin, I used the stopper to seal the bottle tight. But my spell was not the only thing that required blood. It was time to leave payment for those who serve me.

I shifted the weight of the body in my arms, letting the head loll back to expose the drying wound. I drew my blade across the faerie's throat, making a second incision. A small trickle of blood flowed and I held the body out to dangle above the icy ground. Blood dripped and pattered onto the cold pavement, forming a steaming puddle.

The last drop of blood fell to the ground and I threw the body in a heap against the wall. My minions would dispose of it later. Holding my gore covered hands to the sky, I laughed. My power was growing and the day of the ritual was fast approaching. I had the tree and the blood. All was going according to plan.

I pulled a sprig of mistletoe from my pocket and flung it at the exsanguinated body. As if bleeding the immortal dry was not enough, the red caps would be certain to feast on its flesh before carrying the remains to the ritual fire. The kiss of death, indeed. I laughed again, walking jauntily away.

As the killer moved further from the blood cooling on the ground, my perspective shifted. I was no longer looking out through the twisted killer's eyes, but the new view wasn't much of an improvement.

Slinking away from the congealing puddle was a beautiful female faerie. She was obviously not afflicted by the cold as she prowled happily with bare feet across the icy ground. Her pale limbs moved with the lithesome grace of a ballerina. The faerie sashayed to a dramatic halt beside the bundle of bones resting on the ground.

She cocked one long finger at the skeleton, beckoning for him to join her. When the skeleton did not respond, because, hello, he was dead as a doornail, the faerie scooped him up into her arms. The cloak fell to the ground as she twirled the naked skeleton in a macabre parody of lively merriment. But the thing she embraced was long dead and the cruel curl of her lips lacked the warmth of happiness.

"Soon all shall witness your talent again, my love," she said. The faerie sighed, tilting her head of brilliant red hair and frowning playfully. "You were always the most gifted of all of my human pets. Now their art appears garish to my eyes and their music discordant to my ears. Return to me, my sweet, and we shall create beauty together once again."

The faerie spun a graceful pirouette, turning her face toward the spot above the blood puddle where my consciousness hovered. I gasped. The otherwise beautiful woman had empty eyes that seemed to radiate blackness darker than the night around us. As she leaned in to gaze at her skeletal lover, lines of darkness spread further across her face.

Whatever spellwork she was dabbling with, it wasn't doing her any favors.

The faerie gave the skeleton a passionate kiss that made my stomach roil then skipped away, melting into the shadows.

I gasped, the killer and her gruesome vision were gone, but I remained trapped within the psychic impressions left on the blood. I was tethered to the dark, red puddle and nothing I tried would cut me free.

That, of course, was when the nightmare vision went from twisted to absolutely terrifying.

One by one, the alley filled with redcaps. They surrounded the puddle of blood, licking their lips with worm-like tongues. I tried again to break free of the vision and failed.

Redcaps normally live in remote locations, within the ruins of old castles and stone towers. In the North East, they had settled along the coast in abandoned lighthouse towers and crumbling civil war fortifications. Redcaps don't normally live in cities, or stray far from their nest, but I had run into one last summer, literally, while walking the streets of Harborsmouth.

My redcap encounter had been in broad daylight, another aberration since the small, dwarflike fae were nocturnal. But that wasn't the most unusual part of that meeting. After wounding me, the redcap had run his tongue along his evil, black blade. But upon tasting my blood, the creature had bowed to me and apologized, even gifting me his dagger as compensation for his actions. He'd run off too quickly for me to get answers, but Kaye still grumbled whenever she looked at that blade. The encounter remained a puzzle.

Redcaps shouldn't be in the city. But now there were a dozen of the vile creatures dipping their hats into the puddle of blood that the female faerie had left behind. These must be her servants, though who knows what redcaps were good for. I really didn't want to know.

Sadly, I had a ringside seat for the show.

Once the redcaps had each soaked their hat in blood, they surrounded the merry dancer's body. An individual with a particularly large hat lifted the sprig of mistletoe from the corpse and dangled it in the air with a mocking grin. Blood ran down his face, from the cap on his head, as he bent down to kiss the dead faerie. The others leaned in as well, looking for all the world as if they were giving the deceased a departing kiss, but when they came away chunks of flesh were missing from the body.

I'd seen enough.

The merry dancer had been killed as part of a blood magic ritual and red caps were involved. I didn't know what it meant, but I did know now what I needed to do. I had to find the faerie mage's lair, and fast.

I fought against the vision, gagging as the image of feasting redcaps swam before me. *Come on Jinx. Get me the Hell out of here.* The redcaps dove their heads back to the body like blood crazed piranha, and I screamed. I fought against the vision, becoming more exhausted as I thrashed against the barriers that had grabbed hold of my mind.

It would be so easy to stop fighting, but giving in to the fatigue and despair was not an option. Not only was being trapped in this vision my worst nightmare, but I was no use to Marvin like this. The kid needed my help. Oh Oberon's eyes, I can't give up now.

My muffled screams turned to moans and whimpers as I returned to myself. I gagged and pulled the scarf from my mouth. Bile rose in my throat and I took a deep breath, but my stomach continued to churn. Heaving, I crawled away from the puddle of blood, now frozen, and vomited up my breakfast. Oh yeah, I was never having flavored coffee again.

"Here," Jinx said. Jinx unsealed a sanitizing wipe packet and handed me the wipe and my gloves. "You okay?"

I didn't feel okay, but nodded anyway. No sense making Jinx worry. My friend had managed to wash the blood from my hands, helping to pull me from my vision. I shuddered. That was one nightmare I never wanted to experience again.

I pulled on my gloves and put a hand to my stomach. I waited for the waves of nausea and dizziness to pass. The headache, apparently, was here to stay. I'd kill for an aspirin, but my pockets were full of charms and weapons, not normal things like aspirin and chewing gum.

I stood slowly and looked around the alley. The filthy street had returned to its pre-vision appearance. No redcaps or crazy homicidal mages—thank Mab.

It was also damned cold.

I rubbed my gloved hands over my arms and stamped my feet against the icy pavement. I winced as the sound echoed up and down the alley. My head felt like it was going to split open and the sound of pixies buzzed in my ear, but we didn't have time to waste. Marvin was missing and I had new information on our killer.

It was time for another visit with our local witch.

CHAPTER 7

"Darkness and light, girl," Kaye said, glowering at me. "When you get yourself into a pickle, you do so with both feet now don't you?" Kaye turned to examine Jinx's injuries, a bloodied knee from a fall on the ice, frown lines deepening. "And you, can't you go one day without harming yourself?"

Jinx winced as Kaye roughly slapped a poultice on her skinned knee. Jinx was always getting injured, and Kaye was a talented herbalist and healer, but the two didn't mix well on a good day. With Kaye grumping about what we discovered in the alley, Jinx had found herself in the hot seat. As soon as Kaye turned her attention to me, Jinx limped away toward the hearth where Hob was pretending not to eavesdrop.

"Someone is killing faeries, and using blood magic...and Marvin is missing," I said, tossing my gloved hands in the air. "What was I supposed to do, go home?"

Kaye sighed, letting go of some of her bluster. The old woman seemed to shrink with the motion, making her look tired and frail.

"You're right, dear," she said. "But Leanansídhe? I didn't think I'd see the day that faerie witch walked into my city. And from what you saw in your vision, she's the reason the redcaps are here too."

I'd met a redcap and knew they were something to fear, especially if the evil dagger-wielding monsters came in large numbers, but Leanansídhe wasn't a name I was familiar with.

"Who, or what, is Leanansídhe?" I asked.

"Leanansídhe is a powerful faerie who lures men with her beauty and the promise of artistic success," Kaye said. "The Fairy Mistress, as she is sometimes known, has appeared throughout history. She is the perfect muse, bringing musicians and artists to new heights."

"But?" I asked.

I knew there was a catch. With faerie magic, there was always a catch.

"She lifts them up, but when they crash, they die," Kaye said, nodding. "Leanansídhe feeds off the frenzied life essence of her artist lovers, causing them to waste away. Not that her pets wouldn't end up dead anyway. Her very presence makes men unstable, especially human males. The talent of these men may burn brightly, but there is a cost to burning a candle at both ends. When Leanansídhe tires of them, as she often does, her pets kill themselves rather than live without her. Leanansídhe is the reason why so many rising talents die young."

The faerie bitch sounded like a succubus, or a psychic vamp with benefits. And now she was acting crazy, or crazier than usual, wanting to bring one of her lovers back from the dead.

"Is she a necromancer?" I asked.

Kaye bit her lip and frowned.

"Not exactly," she said. "Leanansídhe's magic has always been used to improve someone else's creativity. But in some cases, of extreme writer's block for example, it could be said that she brought the artist's talent back from the dead. If her desire is great enough, and she is fueling her magic with blood and amplifying it with mistletoe, then it may be possible. Leanansídhe may indeed have the power to raise the dead."

I shivered, an oily sensation swimming across my gut, as I recalled Leanansídhe slipping her skeletal lover some tongue. Oh yeah, she had plenty of desire alright. I shook my head and tried to remember something helpful from my vision.

"Leanansídhe mentioned 'the tree' and being nearly ready," I said. "Do you think she meant the hamadryad's tree?"

"Yes," she said. "I believe the tree and the timing are just as significant as the blood she's been gathering. What do you know of the winter solstice?"

"Isn't that when you're throwing your nudie party?" Jinx asked. Hob snickered over her shoulder.

I winced, flinching under Kaye's glare.

"It's the pagan holiday that the Christians appropriated for their Christmas, right?" I asked.

"Near enough," she said. "The winter solstice has been celebrated by man since Neolithic times, though the fae and other immortal races have acknowledged the significance of the solstice for millennia. It is the longest night of the year and a time of great magical power. Many have reveled in the darkness, while others have celebrated the winter solstice as a time of rebirth, noting the ever lengthening days that follow in its wake. Whether calling upon the darkness or worshiping the rebirth of the sun, practitioners come together as power gathers."

"So, it would be the perfect time to use dark magic to raise the dead," I said. A night of power, darkness, and rebirth—sounded like a necromancer's wet dream.

"Yes," Kaye said. "If Leanansídhe plans to resurrect her lover, the celestial calendar would be in her favor. There is also the mention of the tree. Many traditions include the burning of the Yule log in winter solstice celebrations. This comes from a very old ritual for harnessing power. In ancient times, a hamadryad's tree was sacrificed to the fire. The tree would burn for twelve days, all the while a spell was cast and animal sacrifices were made, and on the twelfth night the magic was released and the spell complete."

"Are you saying that the Twelve Days of Christmas comes from some tree burning, goat sacrificing ritual?" Jinx asked.

Jinx rolled her eyes, obviously not buying Kaye's story. But I'd seen Kaye's power and perused her library. I believed her.

"Then the murders have all been part of Leanansídhe's plan," I said, putting the pieces together. Finally the killings made sense. "She needed their blood to amplify the spell and their bodies for the sacrificial fire."

Not that there was a lot left of their bodies to sacrifice, after the redcaps filled their bellies.

"And the hamadryad's tree to fuel the fire," Kaye said, nodding. Leanansídhe had killed two faeries with one stone with that murder, gaining the hamadryad for sacrifice and the tree for the ritual fire. "Leanansídhe must be stopped before the twelfth night. Once she is at the pinnacle of her power, the Faerie Mistress will be unstoppable."

Right, and what was to stop the crazy bitch from bringing back all of her dead pets? If she'd been alive for as long as Kaye said, then that was a lot of frenzied lovers. If Leanansídhe wasn't stopped, she'd have an army of zombies by Christmas.

And Marvin could be her next sacrificial lamb.

"What do I need to do?" I asked.

I thrust my chin out and dug in my heels. This Leanansídhe bitch had to be stopped and I was going to be the one to do it. If there was any chance of saving Marvin, then I was all in.

I snuck a glance at Jinx. Worry lines wrinkled her brow, but she nodded. My friend wasn't going to try to talk me out of this job. Good thing, since I'd already decided to rescue Marvin. I wasn't going to let the kid down.

The back door slammed open and we all gasped. Well, speak of the devil.

Jinx yelped and bumped her head on the mantelpiece. Fortunately for her, Hob was too busy staring at the large figure in the doorway to scold her for marring his hearth. I just stood there gaping like a grindylow out of water.

Marvin scratched his cheek and tilted his head to the side as he glanced around the room. His other hand, I noticed, was behind his back. What the heck was going on?

"Marvin, be a dear and explain where you've been," Kaye said. "Ivy has been looking all over the city for you. You were supposed to go shopping together."

Marvin rubbed his head shyly and looked away.

"Sorry, Ivy," he said.

The shock of Marvin being alive, and whole, and *here* was wearing off. I blinked away tears and smiled.

"That's okay, kid," I said. I'm just glad you're alright."

"But where have you been?" Jinx asked, leaning in to examine the troll more closely.

Sweat beaded on Marvin's brow and he stepped back. Marvin looked ready to run.

"Secret," he said, shaking his head.

Marvin had secrets? That was news to me. The kid was like an open book.

"Give us a moment," Kaye said, shooing us away.

Hob slipped down into his home below the hearthstone and I headed out to the hallway. Jinx shrugged and followed. The door closed behind her with a whoosh of magic. Apparently, Kaye wanted some privacy while she interrogated Marvin about where he'd been.

"Think she'll chew him out?" she asked.

"I feel bad for him if she does," I said. "I wouldn't want Kaye mad at me."

"She's not so scary," she said, shrugging and looking at her nails.

"Really?" I asked. "Kaye could destroy your entire shoe collection with the snap of her fingers."

Jinx shuddered. "Okay, that's scary." She slumped against the plain, white wall of the hallway, tilted her head back, and shook thick bangs from her eyes. "Where do you think he was all that time?"

"I don't know," I said with a sigh. "I'm just glad he's safe."

"You going to stick with the case, now that Marvin's back?" she asked.

I thought about lovesick zombies roaming the streets of Harborsmouth, trying to please their Queen.

"Yeah, but you should go home," I said.

"I'm not going home," she said. Jinx pouted and crossed her arms. "I can help."

I tried to think of a reason for Jinx to be somewhere far away from redcaps, blood magic, and a sex crazed faerie muse turned necromancer.

"Think of all the clients we're losing with no one back at the office to answer the phones," I said. Jinx was obsessed with our business success. Maybe that could work to my advantage. "You can switch the lines to take calls from the loft. It'll be safer there..." She frowned at me. "...and you know how Forneus hates our apartment wards."

"True," she said. "I guess I could work from the loft. But are you sure you won't need my help tracking down this Leanansídhe chick?"

"I'm good," I said, crossing my fingers. "I've got Kaye to help me find Leanansídhe, but I need you to hold Private Eye together and keep our clients happy."

"Okay," she said. "But I'm just a phone call away. Ring me if you need anything."

"Sure thing," I said.

Jinx swung her scarf over her shoulder and sauntered away. At the end of the hall she stopped and turned back.

"And if you get yourself killed, I'll be the one using necromancy to bring you back to life, so I can kill you myself," she said.

With a final flip of her hair, Jinx was gone. I let out a sigh of relief. One friend, at least, would be safe. Now it was time to find out why Marvin was keeping secrets. I rapped on the kitchen door and walked back inside.

Kaye loomed over Marvin who sat on a low stool, looking chagrined. I winced and hoped that the lecture was over. I didn't want to get between Kaye and her target.

"Come in, Ivy," Kaye said.

She didn't turn to see who was standing in her kitchen, but somehow she knew it was me. I never knew with Kaye if it was magic or good instincts, but no one can sneak up on her. Not that I've ever tried. I'm impatient, but I'm not suicidal.

I waved to Marvin and leaned against the large plank table that took up most of the hearth side of the room. The kitchen, surrounded by Kaye's magic circle, was modern and bright, but the hearth area reminded me of an old pub. Not surprising with a brownie in charge of domestic duties. In fact, I wondered where the little guy was hiding. The old coot wasn't usually timid—he had a badger's short temper and the mind of an imp.

A flash of brown caught my eye, moving along the shelf by Marvin's elbow. Sneaky little bugger. Marvin was still holding something behind his back and Hob was trying to get a look. I shook my head. Curiosity would get the best of a brownie every time.

"That's enough, Hob," Kaye said, spearing the brownie with her stare. "Now, Marvin, I know you wanted your gift to be a surprise, but Ivy has had a bad day. Perhaps you could give her your present early?"

Hob's eyes bugged out at the mention of a gift, but he remained where he was. *Smart brownie.*

Marvin swallowed and held a small bundle out before him. In his large hand was a beautiful pair of gloves.

"For me?" I asked. I sniffed and wiped at the back of my eyes with my sleeve. Jeesh, the wind had been really cold in that alley. Hopefully I wasn't getting sick.

Marvin nodded and a red hue rose to his cheeks. I stepped forward, but hesitated. Clothing was tricky, since it went against my bare skin, and gloves were the most difficult. If there was a nightmare vision attached to these gloves, I could end up a drooling mess for the holidays. But Marvin was my friend, and I was the closest thing to family the kid had.

I reached out and gingerly lifted the gloves from his palm, trying to smooth a smile across my face.

"Thanks, big guy," I said. I took a deep breath and pulled off the glove I was wearing and slipped one of the new ones on. It fit...like a glove. And there were no horrible visions attached. In fact, there was something about the gloves that felt familiar.

"Marvin went to a lot of trouble to have those made especially for you," Kaye said. "Clurichauns are drunkards and fools, but their tailoring skills rival the infamous cobbler skills of their leprechaun cousins."

I now owned clurichaun crafted gloves? I smiled. That was kind of cool.

"Too drunk for bad thoughts," Marvin said, nodding.

"Yes, clurichauns remain much too inebriated to leave unhappy energy or focused visions on their wares," Kaye said. "And Marvin was clever. He asked Jinx for a piece of leather from an old coat you were donating to Goodwill. That way the material itself would not harm you either."

I always knew that Marvin was smarter than he looked. Now I was convinced the kid was a genius.

"Wow, that's brilliant, Marvin," I said. I flashed the kid a smile. "Thanks. These are the best present ever."

For the first time in years, I actually meant it. Too bad I couldn't revel in the happy moment.

"So," I said, turning to Kaye. "Any idea how I can track down this Leanansídhe bitch before the solstice?"

Unfortunately, Kaye did have an idea. I just didn't like it much. Great, another scary fae to track down. Why does it always have to be a hag?

CHAPTER 8

I kicked a chunk of ice from the edge of the curb and yelped. Taking my frustration out on the frozen landscape wasn't helping. If I hadn't been wearing steel toe boots, I'd be nursing a broken foot.

I stuffed gloved hands into my coat pockets and kept my head down as I continued up the darkening street. I was entering the financial district, a small, but prosperous section of the city hemmed in by corporate glass monstrosities. Looking up at the skyscrapers only gave me vertigo, so I kept my eyes at street level.

The wrought iron and cobbled streets of the Old Port had been replaced by ugly chrome and concrete. Every block of the financial district looked the same with its glossy, high end boutiques, towering law offices, and a Starbucks on every corner.

"We're not in Kansas anymore," I muttered.

"No, you are in Harborsmouth," a familiar voice rumbled from the shadows. "But, then, you knew that already."

I turned to see Forneus emerge from the doorway of a large insurance company. He ran a hand down his expensive suit and fell into step beside me. I sidled away, prepared to run into the sea of rush hour traffic flowing up Congress Street if it meant avoiding his touch.

"What are you doing here?" I asked. I stopped walking and spun to face him, tapping my foot.

"Working," Forneus said. He spread his arms and gestured at the glass and concrete buildings that lined the street. "A demon has to harvest souls somewhere. And contrary to popular belief, lawyers and insurance agents do indeed have souls to sell."

Great. Forneus was down here playing Let's Make A Deal with corporate workaholics while I froze my butt off trying to find a certain faerie hag. Something cold and wet found its way down the neck of my coat and I shivered. It wasn't fair.

As we stood on the sidewalk, snowflakes fell around Forneus, but never managed to land on the demon.

"Don't let Kaye find out you're down here stealing souls," I said. I narrowed my eyes and gripped a silver cross in my gloved hand. In my other pocket, I scooped up a palm full of salt.

"Steal?" he asked. "You wound me deeply, Miss Granger. I can assure you that any deal I make is legally sound."

Yeah, right, and I'm the son of Oberon.

"Look, you were right about the killings," I said. "Someone is murdering faeries. So I don't have time to stand around here and grow icicles. I'll see you around, Forneus."

"Wait," he said. "I know the location of the one you seek."

"Leanansídhe?" I asked.

"Ah, so that is who has been killing faeries," he said. "No, sadly I do not know where to find the Faerie Mistress, but I can lead you to the Winter Hag."

Crap. Forneus had known about the Winter Hag, but not Leanansídhe. Sneaky demon bastard.

"What makes you think I'd trust you?" I asked. "I'm not making a deal for information. No dates with Jinx, remember?"

"You trusted my information about the killer," he said, grinning. "As for the location of The Cailleach, take it as a token of my friendship."

Friendship? With a demon? I laughed.

"You have to be kidding," I said. "What's in it for you, really?"

Forneus sighed and I held my breath as the smell of sulfur filled the street.

"Fine," he said, straightening his tie. "I may have a tidy sum riding on the outcome of this case. But such trivial details do not matter. Find the Winter Hag and stop the killings. She can be found gathering wood and feeding the deer in the park."

Forneus pointed in the direction of Founders Park. When Kaye said she sensed the magic of the Winter Hag in the financial district, I'd never thought to check the park. My friend had described The Cailleach as a strong elemental force who was often referred to as the Queen of Winter, though not to be mistaken with Mab herself. I assumed the hag must have been some corporate president or CEO—an ice queen in her glass tower.

Instead she sounded like one of the homeless who called Founders Park their home.

I turned back to Forneus, but the demon had disappeared. Whatever. I shrugged and hurried down the sidewalk to where Congress Street was bisected by Park Avenue. The financial district had emptied during my talk with Forneus and Park Ave was devoid of any human presence. The only sign of life being the well lit Starbucks on the corner.

I could go for a real cup of coffee, especially after the nasty stuff Jinx had served this morning, but it was already getting late. I needed to find The Cailleach before midnight. Magic users weren't the only ones whose power grew during the Witching Hour and Kaye had warned me that the Winter Hag was a cyclical force that waxed and waned with the seasons and the hours of the day. I wanted information, not to find myself on the receiving end of a transformation spell. Becoming one of The Cailleach's pet deer was not part of my plan.

I shivered and hurried down the street, careful not to slip on the icy sidewalk. Congress Street ran on a high ridge, the backbone of the city. Every street that ran away from Congress slanted steeply downwards, and Park Ave was no exception. As I descended toward the park, the harbor wind at my back ceased.

I scanned the street for assailants then shifted my attention to the park. Crossing the empty street, I warily approached the park entrance. Keeping my charms and makeshift stakes handy, I watched the trees for movement, but the only motion came from flickering shadows beneath a humming streetlight.

Lengthening shadows reached like skeletal fingers as the sun began to set behind the trees. I clutched the iron nails in my pocket and crept forward on the balls of my feet. I searched the darkness below the trees one more time and, satisfied that nothing supernatural lurked there, stepped onto the frozen grass. The gates hung open like a yawning grave and nothing stirred as I entered Founders Park.

It was like entering another world.

The sounds of city life drifted away, replaced by dead air. A heavy silence smothered the park, broken only by a high pitched squeak as a hunched figure came toward me pushing a rusty shopping cart. The sun retreated and the ice covered pond snapped as a thick layer of frozen water shifted. I jumped and the old crone cackled.

I had found The Cailleach.

I cleared my throat and stepped into a pool of light cast by the flickering street lamp. The hag lifted her head and my stomach heaved. A dark socket was all that was left of her right eye. The other eye stared at me over a large, beaklike nose and her skin was an unhealthy shade of blue. The Cailleach was half my height and her body was bent forward under the weight of a large bundle strapped to her back. The stooped position forced the old crone to twist her neck at an uncomfortable angle to look me in the eye.

The Cailleach was completely unlike the water hags I'd dealt with in the past. Hopefully that meant she was less crazy than her swamp dwelling cousins.

The Winter Hag lifted a bag of dried corn and flashed a toothless grin.

"Hungry?" she asked.

The old crone was trying to feed me deer food? Okay, maybe she was mad as a hatter.

"Um, no thanks," I said.

I shuffled my feet wondering how to begin. Asking faerie favors was tricky. A faerie bargain was binding and immortality gave the fae a long time to practice their deal making skills. I had learned the hard way that faeries will always get the upper hand. The trick wasn't winning so much as surviving.

And I didn't have time for haggling.

"Too bad," she said. The Cailleach sighed and tucked the bag of corn into the folds of her rag dress. "You would have made a lovely pet."

Mab's bones, she really did want to turn me into one of her pet deer. My chest tightened and I struggled to breathe normally. This wasn't the time for a panic attack. I shook my head and focused on the job. I needed to learn the location of Leanansídhe's lair and get the hell out of Dodge.

"I can bring you more deer food, for information on where I can find Leanansídhe," I said.

I planted my feet hip width apart and took a deep breath. My gloved hands were cramping, but I held tightly to my anti-fae charms. If this went down badly, I'd have to fight or run.

The Cailleach rummaged through her cart, finally finding whatever it was she was looking for.

"This will lead you to the Faerie Mistress," she said. She held out a hotel key in a gnarled hand. "But human food will not sate my pets. If you wish to strike this bargain, I require a branch from the hamadryad's tree. Fetch me a branch before the Yule log fully burns or face my wrath. That is my offer."

Crap, what were the odds that I could do as she asked? But what choice did I have? I needed to find Leanansídhe before she unleashed her zombie lovers on the world. Talk about a Christmas gift from Hell. I lifted my chin and nodded curtly.

"Deal," I said.

The hag raised her hand and cackled, the laugh ending in a phlegm filled cough. The hotel key fell to the frost covered ground. With a squeak of the rusty cart, The Cailleach lurched away, the bundle of sticks on her back rocking to and fro as she shuffled deeper into the park.

Was the key the clue, or did it require a vision? I skirted the key like a viper, finally hunching down and slipping a glitter topped pencil from my belt. I slid the pencil through the key ring and lifted it to the streetlight. A fancy crest and the words "Bishop Hotel" gleamed dully in the flickering light. I'd sniff around there and see if anyone had seen any suspicious activity. Maybe the Faerie Mistress was staying there and the key led to Leanansídhe's room.

It was a start.

CHAPTER 9

One thing was painfully obvious as I strode up the steps of the Bishop Hotel. No one had occupied a room here in years. The door hung open, the frame swollen and warped from damp and disuse.

I pushed the door open wider with the toe of my boot and peeked inside. Black mold climbed the walls, marring the elaborate wallpaper and draperies. The lobby was lit only by light from the street lamps outside that filtered in through the open door and a broken window gaping above a second floor balcony.

I flicked on a mini maglite and shone it around the room. The floor looked sound, though I avoided the decaying carpet runner as I stepped into the room. I covered my face with a gloved hand and stifled a sneeze. Dust rose in amber clouds as I tiptoed further into the hotel lobby.

I shone my light along the floor where small feet had walked back and forth through the dust, a large object dragged between them. Someone, probably Leanansídhe's redcap henchmen, had been here recently.

I followed the tracks, careful not to make a sound as I walked past a marble counter and into a dark service passage. The hallway was wide, but unadorned. An old laundry cart stood beside a metal door farther down the hall to my right and a storeroom spilling its contents into the corridor was to my left.

I stepped over the abandoned bottles of cleaner and rolls of toilet paper that prior thieves hadn't wanted and followed the dusty prints down the hall toward the laundry cart. I stood on tiptoe and peered inside the small window inset into the metal door. Stairs led down into impermeable darkness.

Great, it looked like the redcaps were holing up in the basement. I reached out with a gloved hand and tried the doorknob, surprised when it turned easily. I turned my head to the side and examined the door. It wasn't locked. Leanansídhe was either sloppy or confident that she and her redcaps could deal with any intruders.

Or maybe the faerie was just too crazy to care.

My stomach tensed and I forced myself into motion. Standing in the spooky old hallway wasn't doing me any good. Plus, I had to locate the hamadryad's tree, and remove a branch for The Cailleach, before it burned completely. Sadly, amorous zombies weren't my only worry. If Leanansídhe was successful, and the Yule log burned to ash, I'd have no way of fulfilling my end of the bargain with the Winter Hag. I shivered, icy fingers trailing up and down my spine. That was one old crone I didn't want to break a deal with.

I pulled the metal door open and let the narrow beam from my flashlight shine down the stairway. I gasped and lurched back, distancing myself from the mass of spider webs that clung to the ceiling and walls. The redcaps had come this way, but they were pint sized compared to my height. The webs had only been cleared as high as my knees.

Why did it always have to be spiders?

A memory of the spider "cloth merchant" on Joysen Hill crept in unbidden. The carnivorous faerie had used his glamour to cover his terrifying visage, and the bodies of his prey, from human eyes. Unfortunately for me, my second sight allowed me to cut through his glamour to see the men and women wrapped in spider silk, hanging from the fire escape above his market stall. The image of wriggling human-sized snacks dangling above the spider faerie had haunted my dreams for weeks.

I swallowed hard and rubbed my gloved hands along my arms. I could do this. There were no man eating spider fae here. It was just a bunch of old cobwebs, right? I took a shuddering breath and crept down the stairs, moving as fast as I could without alerting the entire basement of my presence.

"It's just cotton candy," I muttered.

Something skittered along a web to my left and I cringed. I pulled the collar of my coat up higher and kept moving. At the bottom of the stairs I took a shuddering breath and shook web from my hands and hair.

Waiting for my eyes to adjust to the dim light, I studied the smells of mildew, wood smoke, and decay. A hint of detergent hung on the air and I realized the large objects to my far left were washing machines. My eyes continued to adjust to the darkness and I confirmed that this was the laundry room for the hotel. Industrial washers and dryers lined one wall and a large steamer sat like a metal gargoyle in the center of the room.

I crouched down and circuited the steamer and folding tables. Something let out a raucous laugh and tinny chamber music played in the room beyond. I froze, but when no one came looking for me, I continued forward.

Beyond the laundry room was a cavernous space. The walls were rough brick lined with exposed plumbing and wiring for the hotel above. A large furnace was the focal point of the room. The metal beast billowed smoke where it rose from the dirt floor, but someone had tried to make the place homey—if you lived in a Victorian parlor.

I inched further into the room, keeping to the shadows, to get a better view. Velvet fainting couches lined the walls beside small tables covered in doilies and photographs of people sleeping. In coffins? Scratch that, they weren't sleeping. The people in the gilt frames were dead. That wasn't creepy or anything.

But the creep factor didn't stop there. Redcaps surrounded the large furnace. The door of the furnace hung open, a large tree protruding from its fiery maw. The redcaps looked like red ants climbing up and down a series of ropes to where a metal spit hung over the burning tree. Taking turns, the redcaps cranked a lever, turning the items on the spit over and over again.

My stomach roiled and I looked away. The dead faeries—peri, hamadryad, pixie, Fear Dearg, and the merry dancer—hung from the spit as it slowly rotated over the fire. Bile rose in my throat and I swallowed hard. The redcaps giggled with glee each time the bodies snapped and popped above the fire, as if eagerly awaiting a Christmas roast.

I blinked away tears from the lingering smoke haze and scanned the room for additional threats. There, sitting on a striped satin fainting couch was Leanansídhe and her dead lover. The Faerie Mistress cradled the skeleton in her arms, relishing in his embrace. She lifted an athame, ritual dagger, in one hand and dragged it along the skeleton's cheek, then leaned in for a kiss. The macabre tableau made my stomach twist and I felt my skin crawl.

Leanansídhe was most definitely unhinged. As Hob once explained to me, the very, very old fae tended to go through an unhealthy stage of boredom that was often followed by a period of "goin' doololly." Some fae manage to retrieve their sanity again over time, but most remained damaged. I thought Jinx put it best when I explained my earlier vision of the Faerie Mistress. Leanansídhe was fuck nuts crazy.

With the powerful faerie and her pets surrounding the Yule log, there was no way that I could retrieve The Cailleach's branch, remove the bodies from the roasting spit, pull the hamadryad's tree from the fire, and put an end to the power fueling the necromancy spell. I needed more firepower.

It was time to call Jenna.

I crept back toward the entrance, holding my breath as I crab-walked back the way I came. I bit my lip, back muscles straining, as I inched forward, careful not to bump the table holding the gramophone. Making the music skip would definitely catch Leanansídhe's attention.

My boots touched concrete and I let out a shaky breath. I'd made it to the laundry room. I risked a glance back to the cavernous room behind me to see the Faerie Mistress continuing to stroke the cheek of her skeleton lover. For now, at least, I was safe.

I scanned the laundry room for threats then inched to the basement stairs. Looking up through the tunnel of spider webs, the door to the hotel looked far away. But I couldn't risk making the call here. I needed to escape the basement level where I might be overheard.

Pulling my coat tight around my neck, I put one foot on the step, then another. I was nearly at the door, my hand reaching for the handle, when a stair tread let out a loud squeak of protest. I lifted my foot and froze. Had I given myself away?

I held my breath and counted to twenty. Sticky webs tickled my nose and something skittered along my coat sleeve. An itch burned between my shoulder blades, but I didn't turn around. When I was sure that there were no footsteps approaching from behind me, I crept up the last few stairs and pushed out into the hotel service corridor.

With trembling hands, I closed the metal door and leaned against it. Mab's bones, that was close. I closed my eyes and took a steadying breath. I made a mental note of which stair had had the squeaky tread and pushed away from the wall.

It was time to call in reinforcements.

I punched in Jenna's number from memory. The petite, young Hunter had helped me on a few cases since we'd met last summer. We weren't exactly friends—she killed faeries for a living and I was a wisp half breed—but I'd earned her respect that first night on the waterfront. I had been ready to die to save innocent humans from supernatural baddies and that was what all Hunters were sworn to do. I may not be fully human myself, but I fit with Jenna's ideals. So far that worked for both of us.

"Got a case?" Jenna asked. Her breathless voice came down the line in bits and pieces between the rhythmic clang of metal on metal. She must have been in the sparring room at the Guild's home base, where Hunters trained obsessively. "Just a sec." The background noise ceased and Jenna let out a barking laugh. "Need help with another gnome infestation?"

I grimaced. Jenna had helped me net a small family of gnomes long enough to warn them that the empty lot where they lived was being turned into a shopping mall. My client had hired me to serve the eviction notice. It had sounded like a straightforward job, but the gnomes had cried and pleaded with me. It hadn't been my finest moment.

"Not gnomes, redcaps," I said, keeping my voice low. "And a faerie necromancer. I'm at the old Bishop Hotel on Forsythe. Leanansídhe and her redcap minions are down in the basement. I need to stop a blood magic spell that she's casting, but so far they've only harmed other faeries..."

"So the Guild won't help on this one," she said.

The Hunters Guild only helped fight against faeries to protect humans. Since Leanansídhe hadn't hurt any humans yet, their hands were tied. But Jenna wasn't opposed to the occasional side job. She said it kept her skills sharp.

Personally, I didn't think Jenna needed the practice, but I was always happy to have her help. I kept in shape and went through a series of self defense moves each evening while Jinx made dinner, but I used speed and surprise to disarm and run away from my attackers. Hand to hand combat was no good when the brush of skin on skin could mean crippling visions. Jenna had offered to teach me how to handle a blade, but even the thought of holding a weapon made my stomach hurt.

"Right, the Guild isn't an option," I said. "Are you in?"

"Be there in five," she said. "And Ivy? Don't do anything foolish before I get there."

I considered the basement full of bloodthirsty redcaps and their crazy, magic using faerie leader.

"That won't be a problem," I said. "I'll wait for you in the lobby."

CHAPTER 10

Five minutes seemed to take an eternity, but Jenna arrived on schedule. She may spend most of her time plotting to kill faeries, but Jenna was punctual. You had to give her that.

"We have approximately nine redcaps here," Jenna said. She made a mark in the dust that covered the lobby floor. "And you last saw the faerie mage here."

"Yes," I said, nodding at the hasty diagram.

"Okay," she said. "You go in first and I'll bring up the rear. Get as close to the furnace as you can, without the redcaps seeing you. Once you're in close, I'll create a distraction. Run to the Yule log and retrieve the branch you need from the tree. After securing the branch, hit the emergency shutdown switch here. That should cut off the oil supply, but with wood to fuel the fire, the tree will probably continue to burn. Loop the rope around the tree and try to pull it from the furnace. I'll come over and help once I incapacitate the enemy."

Jenna made it sound easy, but I had a bad feeling that we were taking on something too big for just the two of us. I was tempted to call Kaye for magical support, but shook away the thought. The fight on the waterfront had weakened Kaye physically and diminished her power. I thought of the black lines snaking down my friend's arms to encircle her wrists and hands. I sat up straight and clenched my fist. No, I wasn't going to put Kaye in danger again. She may not survive another magic battle. Jenna and I would have to do this on our own.

"Anything else?" I asked.

"If you see anything hiding beneath a glamour that I don't, text me," she said. "I'll have my phone on vibrate. If it looks like I'm about to walk into a glamoured trap, scream like bloody murder. Otherwise, stick with the plan."

Jenna didn't have my gift of second sight, but Hunters don't run blindly into battle. Jenna's eyelids shone with a greasy substance she'd rubbed on when she got here. Faerie ointment didn't work as well as second sight, but it did help humans see glamoured fae.

The scent of faerie ointment—clover, periwinkle, culver's keys, forget-me-nots, primrose, and thyme—reminded me of Jinx. Kaye had whipped up a batch when our clientele had changed. Being able to tell if the person walking through your office door was a creature that may want to eat you tended to be helpful, though Jinx applied hers with a makeup brush. Jenna looked like she was suffering from a bad case of conjunctivitis.

I felt a pang of guilt when I thought about my roommate. I hadn't called Jinx to tell her that I'd found Leanansídhe's lair. My friend would have rushed here in an effort to keep me safe. Jinx was tough, but she wasn't a Hunter. It was better that she was safe back at the loft. Now we just had to stop the bad guys and keep her that way.

"Okay, ready when you are," I said.

I brushed dust from my knees and led Jenna down the service corridor. Having a sudden idea, I stopped at the open supply closet and poked my head inside. There on the bottom shelf was a first aid kit and a fire extinguisher. I moved the first aid kit, and a stack of towels, out into the hallway where we might need them later. The fire extinguisher I lifted up to show Jenna and grinned.

"What do you think?" I asked. "If I douse the wood after hitting the manual shut off for the furnace, this should put the fire out. We may not have to pull the Yule log out of the furnace."

I'd been worrying about that detail. I wanted to zip in and out, foiling the Faerie Mistress' plans by ruining her spell. If I didn't have to waste time dragging an entire tree from a furnace, I'd have a chance to save the remains of the faeries who had died at the hands of Leanansídhe and her redcap cronies.

"Check the last charge date," she said.

I turned the extinguisher over and, miraculously, it hadn't expired. The propellant and fire retardant were good for another month.

"Looks good," I said.

"Then bring it," she said. "If it gets too unwieldy, leave it and keep moving. Stealth will be the most important thing.

You need to get close to the furnace before I begin my diversion."

I nodded, patting the fire extinguisher and tucking it under my arm. I went to the metal basement door and peeked through the tiny window pane to the stairs below. I didn't shine my flashlight this time. It was dark, but I couldn't detect any movement on the stairs.

I pulled the door open and began my descent, careful to avoid the squeaky step. Jenna followed my lead and I turned my attention back to the shadowy basement below. Once we'd cleared the stairs, I crouched low and crab-walked through the laundry room. I passed the looming steamer press with Jenna at my back. So far, so good.

My boots hit dirt and I peered around the corner into the cavernous room beyond. I bit my lip and scanned the room for faeries. Leanansídhe was dancing with her skeleton in the center of the dirt floor. But where were the redcaps?

I jumped at the loud squeal of rusting hinges as the door of every washer and dryer snapped opened behind us. Teeth and daggers gleamed red in the faint firelight as redcaps emerged from where they'd been hiding inside the bellies of the machines. Oh Oberon's eyes, we had walked into a redcap ambush.

I froze, watching redcaps pour out of the machines like spiders in a rainstorm. For creatures with short, stubby legs, they sure could move fast.

Jenna spun on her heel to face our ambushers and shouted, "Ivy, go!"

I launched out of my crouch, stealth no longer an option, and ran toward the burning Yule log. We had abandoned our original plan, forced by the attack to improvise, but my goal remained the same. I had to shut down the furnace and stop the tree from burning.

With no redcaps in my path, I sprinted past the gramophone and over an ornate fainting couch. The sounds of battle raged behind me, but I couldn't risk looking over my shoulder. I had to stick with my goal. But redcaps were nasty little creatures and I hoped that Jenna would be able to fight them off long enough for me to disrupt Leanansídhe's spell.

I smiled as I heard the *thwap, thwap* of Jenna's crossbow, followed by a ragged scream. The Hunter had hit one of the redcaps with an iron bolt. That was one bloodthirsty faerie who wouldn't be continuing this fight. One redcap down, seven more to go.

The furnace grew larger as I made my way across the room and my chest lightened. Calling Jenna had been the right decision. The clang of her sword rang out and another redcap wailed. We were going to shut this spell down and save the day. No more innocent faeries were going to die. Not in my city.

I grinned, showing my teeth, and increased my speed. My thighs were burning, but I was nearly there. All those morning runs along the waterfront were finally paying off.

A low muttering echoed against the walls off to my right and my grin faltered. Leanansídhe had lowered her skeleton dance partner to the ground and her lips moved rapidly as she recited an incantation. Crap, that was never a good sign.

I turned to see if help was on the way, but Jenna had her hands full with the redcaps.
Their bloodlust had reached a frenzied pitch at the bloodletting of their comrades. The redcaps were climbing over the bodies of their fallen to encircle Jenna. Mab's bloody bones.

I was on my own.

I veered to the right, toward Leanansídhe. I couldn't outrun a spell, but maybe I could toss a monkey wrench into the works. And when you don't have a monkey wrench, a fire extinguisher will do.

I hooked the gloved fingers of my left hand under the spray nozzle and slapped my right hand on the back of the red metal tank. Swinging the fire extinguisher in an arc, I used my momentum to smash the Faerie Mistress in the head—and kept on running.

A jolt of pain ran up my arms, but I retained my grip on the metal canister. I still needed the fire extinguisher if I hoped to put out the flames that continued to eat away at the Yule log. Plus, I might need it again for more head bashing.

I risked a glance over my shoulder as I continued my run for the furnace. Leanansídhe was still standing, but she had stopped mouthing the words of her spell. Knowing it wouldn't last long, I used the brief reprieve to bolt forward and hit the emergency power shutoff button on the side of the furnace.

I wiped tearing eyes with the backs of my gloves and headed into the thick smoke surrounding the Yule log. Pulling my scarf around my nose and mouth, I peered through the haze looking for a branch for The Cailleach.

A scream rang out from behind me, but I focused on what was left of the hamadryad's tree. There, toward the end of the burning log, one branch remained. The tips of the winter-dry branch were beginning to curl in the heat, but it was whole. I breathed a sigh of relief. Surviving this only to be struck down by the Winter Hag would suck, big time.

Leanansídhe's guttural muttering began again and I hurried forward. I brushed sparks from my coat and reached over the blackened tree trunk to grab the branch. I gripped the base of the branch with both gloved hands, but flames roared as the Faerie Mistress pulled power from the burning Yule log to fuel her spell.

No! I fell backward, blinking my eyes against the flames that shot three feet into the air. The hamadryad's tree was burning faster and the remaining branch had caught fire. I had to douse the flames. The burning Yule log and the blood sacrifices hanging above were lending power to Leanansídhe's magic.

The branch would have to wait.

I raised the fire extinguisher and aimed it at the center of the blaze. Once the flames within the furnace began to dim, I swung the extinguisher back toward the burning branch before resuming my attempt to extinguish the flames.

I sensed movement, grabbed a handful of iron shavings from my pocket and flung them at the ground behind me. If it was Jenna the iron wouldn't do her any harm, but the iron would burn any pureblood fae. Judging by the screams, it hadn't been my human friend.

I continued to aim the fire extinguisher at the furnace until, with a final puff and fizzle, the device ran dry. I couldn't see through the cloud of smoke, foam, and white powder, but I heard a growl to my left.

I ducked and rolled beneath the Yule log, where it protruded from the furnace, holding the fire extinguisher to my chest. The growling followed me beneath the tree and I sprung to my feet the moment I'd cleared it, and swung the metal canister at knee height—right at head level, for a redcap. I nearly took the redcap's head off as he ran at the oncoming battering ram.

The redcap's eyes rolled up into his skull as he fell over backward. I lifted the fire extinguisher onto my shoulder and reached inside my coat. I withdrew a packet of powdered mandrake root and sprinkled it over the burning tree and onto the floor below. It wouldn't stop the full force of Leanansídhe's spells, but any protection against black magic was welcome at this point.

I kicked the redcap, making sure he was out cold, and surveyed the battle. The room had filled with smoke, making it difficult to pick out friend or foe. But I couldn't feel the electric tingle that often accompanied powerful magic.

I moved back toward where I'd last seen the burning branch, crossing my fingers. If I didn't have a branch for The Cailleach, I'd be up an *each uisge* filled creek.

I squinted through the smoke and brushed away the thick layer of foam and white powder that coated the tree, trunk and branch. Had the remaining branch burned? It was time to find out. I set the fire extinguisher on the ground at my feet and reached forward with shaking hands.

My gloved hands found the slender wood sprouting from the log and brushed away the last of the powder. Brown and gray bark emerged—the branch was intact. I snapped the branch from the tree, wrapped it in my scarf, and tucked it into my belt. The branch created a large bulge beneath my coat, but I wasn't going to leave it here. I patted the bundle and smiled.

I could live to fight another day.

The Cailleach may let me live, but I was sure the redcaps and their mistress had other ideas—if they were still alive. Boots crunched on iron shavings and I grabbed two stakes from my belt. They may not work as well on fae as they would with vamps, but I could certainly slow down a redcap if I jammed a stake in its eye.

I strained my hearing and held my breath. I blinked away tears, but couldn't see anything through the heavy smoke. The steps continued toward me, sounding light and graceful. I lifted my arm higher and adjusted my grip on the stake. That didn't sound like an approaching redcap.

I counted—one one thousand, two one thousand, three one thousand—and swung my right arm, ready to follow up with my left. A hand lashed out and grabbed my wrist in its iron grip and I tensed, sucking air through my teeth. Receiving a vision from Leanansídhe could fry my brain. I remembered Kaye reciting the immortal Faerie Mistress' long line of pet artists. Leanansídhe had left thousands of corpses in her wake. I bit the inside of my cheek, tamping down my panic. If given the choice, I'd rather face her magic.

The scent of primrose and thyme met my nose and I slumped forward. I loosened my grip on the stakes and locked my knees, trying not to slide to the floor. My legs had gone wobbly, and stars danced on the edge of my vision, but the Hunter's face emerged from the smoke haze.

"Jenna?" I asked.

"If I'd been the Faerie Mistress, you'd be dead right now," Jenna said. She shook her head and let go of my wrist. "You really need to reconsider my offer for weapons training."

I let out a shaky laugh and brushed a piece of falling ash from my cheek. Jenna had a point. I caught a glimpse of my gloves and winced. I was lucky that my hands weren't covered in third degree burns. My leather gloves were a charred mess. Good thing Marvin had given me new ones for Christmas. I'd have to make sure and thank the kid.

"You may be right," I said. "So where is Leanansídhe?"

Jenna pointed to the ground a few feet away. The faerie was sitting in the dirt, rocking the skeleton she held in her arms. A low moaning rose from her mouth and Leanansídhe began sobbing into the skeleton's shoulder.

"Must hear him play again…such beautiful music," she cried.

I almost felt bad for her. My eyes rose to the small bodies hanging from the spit above the blackened tree. The bodies were charred and covered in bite marks from where Leanansídhe had encouraged the redcaps to feed. Maybe she didn't deserve my pity. I limped to a dainty, velvet armchair and pulled it over to the furnace.

"What do we do with her?" Jenna asked.

Jenna pulled her crossbow from her back and aimed it at the insane faerie. I shrugged. I didn't have a lot of sympathy for Leanansídhe. She'd killed….for her own greed. But she was obviously unhinged. I thought back to the number of times I had come close to losing my own sanity.

Jenna began pulling the bow string back and I shook my head. I may not like the faerie witch, especially now that I was standing eye to eye with her roasted victims, but the woman was clearly insane.

"Wait," I said, raising a smoking hand. "Let me call Kaye. She'll know what to do."

Jenna went back to guarding Leanansídhe and I struggled to dial The Emporium with scorched gloves. Kaye wasn't thrilled at my suggestion to keep the faerie alive, but eventually she caved in. She knew a Ghillie Dhu who ran a faerie rehab containment facility outside Boston. I was fuzzy on the details, but the important thing was Kaye agreed to make the necessary calls and get Leanansídhe into the facility before dawn. It may have been kinder to kill the faerie, but at least I wouldn't be responsible for her death.

I'd do almost anything to protect my friends and keep the city safe, but I wasn't comfortable with the role of executioner. And if I agreed to let Jenna kill Leanansídhe, that's exactly what I'd be. It didn't matter which of us pulled the trigger.

While talking to Kaye on speakerphone, I worked at removing the dead bodies from the metal spit. I had trudged back up the basement stairs and retrieved the first aid kit and towels from the hotel service corridor. I now had my gloved hands and arms wrapped in towels monogrammed with the BH of the Bishop Hotel. My entire body shook, but I swallowed my fear of nightmare visions and finished the job. Talking with Kaye helped to keep me distracted.

I used gauze from the first aid kit and more towels as shrouds, wrapping each of the burned bodies before setting them on one of the fancy couches that lined the walls. It was hard work, wrapping the faeries with my own clumsy, towel wrapped hands. But they deserved this token of respect. I would make sure that each of the bodies was returned to their people and laid to rest in the manner in which they would wish. It seemed like the least I could do.

I hadn't been able to protect these faeries, but I swore that no more innocents, fae or human, would go unnoticed in my city. Not on my watch. And if I was going to be protecting the residents of Harborsmouth, I needed more training.

"Jenna, that offer for weapons training still stand?" I asked.

Jenna wasn't cheap, but I could give myself training sessions for Christmas. Maybe Jinx would like lessons as well.

She was getting feisty with her sharpened crosses and holy water grenades. Making ourselves kick ass for the New Year? Sounded like a resolution to me.

Of course, I'd still have to get Jinx a new pair of shoes. Either that or I'd be the first person she'd stake.

EPILOGUE

My hand twitched as the Felix the Cat clock ticked on the kitchen wall. I scowled at the time and grabbed my shawl from the granite counter, shaking my head. I had hoped that Ceff would be here to escort me to Kaye's crappy solstice party, but he hadn't showed. The kelpie and selkie negotiations must not be going well.

I stomped to the door, and flicked off the overhead lights. I stood in the glow of the city lights that filtered in through the loft windows and took a steadying breath. Jinx had gone on ahead with her date while I insisted on waiting for Ceff.

I should have gone with Jinx and Hans, but I felt like a third wheel and I still wasn't thrilled about Jinx going on a date with the Hunter. Hans was trouble, but then again so was Jinx. I shook my head. At least she wasn't going with Forneus. The demon had sent numerous requests to be her date, but Jinx had refused. At least attending the party on the arm of a skilled Hunter meant that Jinx wouldn't be bothered by the demon tonight. I sighed and leaned against the cool metal of our apartment door.

I'd have to walk into Kaye's party on my own.

I was used to being a loner, but walking into a nude dance party, rife with magic circles and group orgies, had me checking my body for weapons. The dress I'd worn, since I wasn't going to tear off my clothes and run naked under the solstice moon, didn't have as many places for stashing stakes and blades as I'd like. How did Jinx manage to hide all of those sharpened crosses in her skirts?

I snorted, remembering Jinx's last attempt to stab Forneus. Jinx and I had started taking lessons with our Hunter friend Jenna and the training sessions had paid in spades. Too bad demons like the rough stuff. Jinx was never going to rid herself of Forneus now.

I tipped my head back and stared at the ceiling. Maybe I'd feel better after a walk under the stars. Starlight soothed my wisp half and the walk might calm my jangled nerves. If not, I could stop on the way for some liquid courage. The streets between our apartment and The Emporium were lined with bars and it was late on a Wednesday night. I might be able to duck in and out without anyone trying to touch me. And if they tried, I'd have an excuse to use some of the moves Jenna was teaching me.

I grinned, showing my teeth, and pulled the door open. Ceff stood startled on the top landing. His hand was lifted, as if to knock on the door. I gasped and stepped back, but the grin didn't leave my face.

"You made it," I said, looking him over.

Ceff looked dapper in a suit and tie, but if you looked past his faerie glamour he wasn't wearing shoes. Apparently kelpie kings prefer to go around barefoot, even in winter. I glanced up in time to see Ceff looking me over as well. I blushed, running a hand down the shimmering dress. I had planned on wearing pants and a turtleneck, but Jinx had insisted on the evening gown.

"You look stunning in that dress," he said.

Ceff stepped inside, careful to keep his distance, and looked around the darkened room. He raised an eyebrow and I nodded.

"Jinx already left for the party," I said. "I was just..."

"Working up your courage?" he asked.

We hadn't been dating for very long, but Ceff knew me well. He was one of the few people I trusted enough to let my guard down with. I enjoyed being able to just be myself around Ceff. I smiled and gestured to the couch.

I sat at one end of the couch and turned on the table lamp. I knew that Ceff's eyes could see well enough in the dark, and my night vision was rapidly improving as my wisp abilities matured, but the darkness seemed too intimate. I sighed, folding my gloved hands in my lap, and perched on the edge of the couch. Jinx was right. I had issues.

"I have something for you," Ceff said.

He pulled a small, beribboned box from his pocket and set it on the couch between us. My Christmas present? But it wasn't Christmas yet.

I hesitated, hand shaking, as I leaned toward the package. Gifts made me nervous and the tiny box before me was no exception. But I didn't want to hurt Ceff's feelings. He looked so eager. I took a steadying breath and reached for the box.

I pulled the ribbon away and lifted the lid with the tips of my gloves. A seaweed covered item rested inside. Please say that wasn't jewelry, or a hat. Jinx would laugh for a week if she saw me wearing seaweed. Ceff cleared his throat and smiled.

"This was a boon from the selkie queen, the payment for my recent services to aid in the negotiations with her people," he said. Ceff's voice trickled over me like water, but I forced myself to pay attention to his words. "It grants the recipient one night without visions. She claimed that it was crafted with powerful magic at the request of a clairvoyant. How it came under the selkie queen's possession, I do not know."

Wait, a night without visions? But that meant...

"I could touch you," I said, a blush rising to burn my cheeks.

"Yes, but it is up to you how you wish to use it," he said.

He was saying that I didn't have to use the item to touch him, but Ceff looked pleased. I looked around the empty room. Jinx was at the party and would be dancing with Hans until dawn. I smiled a wicked grin, feeling giddy with excitement. Ceff had given me the best gift ever.

I reached for the magic seaweed and turned off the lamp.

GHOST LIGHT SNEAK PEEK

Keep reading the award-winning Ivy Granger series.

Ghost Light (Ivy Granger #2) by E.J. Stevens

Now Available

Trade Paperback . Ebook . Audiobook

CHAPTER 1

What do the names g*host light, friar's lantern, corpse candle, aleya, hobby lantern, chir batti, faerie fire, min min light, luz mala, spook light, ignus fatuus, orbs, boitatá,* and *hinkypunk* have in common? They are all names for wisps. Corpse candle? Now that was bound to give a girl a complex.

I had recently discovered that I was half fae. My faerie half is wisp, as in Will-o'-the-Wisp—my father, king of the wisps. It was a lot to digest.

Dealing with my newfound princess-of-the-wisps status was stressful, but business was booming and I didn't have time for random panic attacks. I used to see a therapist to help deal with my anxiety. Lately, I visited Galliel at Sacred Heart church.

Galliel wasn't the priest at Sacred Heart, though I usually stopped and said hello to Father Michael while there. Father Michael had helped me with my recent demon trouble, but spending time with him didn't relieve my anxiety like Galliel did. It wasn't Father Michael's fault. He was a good priest, as far as I could tell, but he was only human. Galliel was a unicorn.

I was indulging in my guilty pleasure, Galliel's adoring head resting in my lap, while Ceff spoke with the priest. This was bliss. I had always wondered what true happiness was like, but never thought I'd have the opportunity to experience it for myself. Somehow, during a catastrophic week that nearly brought my city to its knees, I had found my own. Galliel was a big part of that. So was Ceff.

If I were looking for love on Craig's List, my singles ad would begin something like, "Must Love Unicorns." Of course, I didn't have to look for love online. My heart now belonged to Ceff.

Ceffyl Dŵr, or Ceff, was a kelpie. In fact, he was king of the local kelpies. Since discovering my wisp princess birthright, that seemed somewhat fortuitous. It was also extremely dangerous. The kelpie king had plenty of enemies. He also had a murderous, sociopathic wife.

I didn't care. For the first time in my life, I felt like I truly belonged. I had so much to be thankful for; a gorgeous date; an amazing best friend, business partner, and roommate; a wonderful mentor; fabulous new friends; numerous clients; and a pet freaking unicorn.

I should have known that something bad was coming. I have said it before and I'll say it again; Fate is a fickle bitch.

*****

Most people have skeletons in their closets. I wasn't born yesterday, and I am fully aware that my boyfriend was born more yesterdays ago than I can count. Since Ceff is a few millennia old, I expect some dusty bones lurking behind the perfectly pressed shirts, faded jeans, and tailored suits—no shoes of course. What I didn't expect was for Ceff's skeletons to come storming from the dark corners of his closet with finger bones raised in anticipation of clawing my eyes out.

Ceff was married once. To put it nicely, the woman was a freaking bitch. I'd say the chick was a harpy, but that would insult harpies everywhere and I didn't want to piss off potential clients. Melusine, Ceff's ex-squeeze and former queen, was pure malicious evil.

Judging from the memories I witnessed in a psychometric vision I had while hunting for Ceff's bridle, the woman was also bat-shit-crazy. Coming from me, that's really saying something. But seriously, what other reason explains a mother murdering her infant child in front of her husband?

Their union, an arranged marriage based on fae politics, may not have been based on love, but Ceff hadn't been a bad husband. He was attentive to his wife and lavished her with gifts befitting a queen. But his true love was reserved for his sons. Unfortunately, that love would spell their doom.

Melusine became so filled with jealousy that she began scheming how to remove her eldest son from his prized role as heir to the kelpie throne. She framed him as a traitor—a crime punishable by death under kelpie law—and watched with glee as her husband meted out the punishment. But her eldest son's public execution was not enough.

Melusine wanted Ceff's love and undivided attention, but even in his grief, Ceff didn't turn to his wife. Instead he shone his affections on his youngest son who was then still just a babe.

Melusine seethed with envy for the love she felt was rightfully hers. What kind of child steals a parent's love from the other? Enraged, she dangled the child over a pit of flames and watched as Ceff struggled to save him. His attempts to plead with her, for the sake of their child, only maddened her further. She threw their baby into the fire and, with a flick of her serpent tail, disappeared into the sea.

I had hoped that the bitch had been eaten by a shark, or run over by a motor boat. Maybe she'd remarried some other poor guy and was making big with the crazy in his ocean. I didn't care, though I was fond of the shark scenario, so long as Melusine was out of the picture.

Too bad she didn't stay that way.

Have you ever taken pictures with friends and everyone is smiling, but when you see the photos later they are dotted with white orbs? Okay, sometimes those are my people, wisps, but more often they appear like ghosts haunting the picture's inhabitants and making the smiles seem grotesque rather than cheerful.

Melusine was like one of those photographic ghosts. She was back in the picture, haunting me and tainting the near-perfect relationship that Ceff and I had with painful memories and the threat of violence. The honeymoon was over before it began—and that really pissed me off.

I'll be turning twenty-five soon and I have never dated anyone until now. I've also never been intimate with anyone. The closest I've come to intimacy was one magical night with Ceff during the winter solstice. Jinx thinks I'm nuts for cuddling on the couch all night when I had the chance for something more, but for me being held was a huge first step. Nearly twenty-five and never been kissed. But I was getting closer to achieving that with Ceff, until his ex-wife showed up.

She better hope she had a leprechaun somewhere in her family tree, because that bitch was going to pay

CLUB NEXUS SNEAK PEEK

Keep reading the award-winning Ivy Granger series.

Club Nexus (Ivy Granger #2.5) by E.J. Stevens

Now Available

Ebook . Audiobook

DEMONIZED

The ogre glared at me from beneath his unfortunate simian brow, waiting for my response. His considerable bulk blocked the entrance to Club Nexus and one sizable hand twitched over the gun strapped to his barrel-like chest. Subtlety was not an ogre's strong suit. Speaking of suits, this creature's taste ran toward pimp chic. The fabric was cheap and shiny, reflecting light from the single working bulb on this street.

"Forneus, Great Marquis of Hell," I said, focusing on the bouncer's beady eyes and avoiding being blinded by his hideous taste in fashion.

The ogre leaned forward, sniffed at the air with a nose the size of a Volkswagen Beetle, and grimaced. *Unpleasant oaf.* Apparently, he didn't care for the aroma of fresh brimstone. Of course, I could mask the sulfurous scent of Hell, but where would be the fun in that? The ogre examined me from head to impeccably dressed toe.

"Don't get many demon lords here," he said, furrowing his substantial brow.

"No, I daresay you wouldn't," I said. "Not with that witch working with the Hunters' Guild to maintain their so-called peace over the entire city of Harborsmouth."

The ogre spat, narrowly missing my shoes. Now it was my turn to grimace. The cretin had utterly appalling manners. Dressing an ogre in a cut-rate suit does not a gentleman make. Before the vile creature could cough up any more distressing substances, I waved toward the door and forced a smile.

"May I enter?" I asked.

A clipboard materialized from thin air, but I was unimpressed. I'd been using the same trick with clients for eons. I tapped my foot, careful to avoid the pile of phlegm that rivaled the size of most cats—perhaps it actually was a cat?—as the ogre consulted his magical guest list.

Finally, the hulking faerie stepped aside and muttered, "You may enter."

I smoothed the front of my waistcoat, tugged at my gloves, and took up my ebony walking stick. The ogre didn't check the polished wood and therefore did not discover the sword hidden within its shaft, which was for the best. Weapons were not entirely forbidden inside the club, just unauthorized bloodshed, but I preferred to keep my secrets. You never know when you'll need a little surprise up your sleeve or, as in this case, inside your perambulatory accessory.

Plus, the hidden blade was made of cold iron. Iron was the one weakness of all fae creatures, a vulnerability that would leave any faerie who touched it powerless. If the ogre tried to handle my sword, he'd get a truly unpleasant surprise.

Hell help any faerie run through with cold iron. The Fair Folk may be immortal, but they are not immune to a painful death. I grinned and walked jauntily past the ogre, into a dark passage and onto an extravagantly wrought spiral staircase where I began my descent into the abyss of otherworldly delights.

From my aerial vantage, I took in the appalling number of fae housed beneath one cavernous roof. Though I rarely grace the establishment with my presence—my last trip below must have been years ago—not much had changed since my earlier visit to the raucous nightclub. Immortals are not fond of change.

Unnatural music wove through the air like dancing phantasms, reaching its spectral fingers into dark places better left untouched. I gritted my teeth and stifled the urge to tap my boots to the discordant rhythm. I searched the room for the woman I'd followed here, an unfamiliar sense of foreboding filling my chest.

It had been centuries since a human had piqued my interest, longer still since anyone had stirred feelings of lust and longing, but there was something unquestionably magnetic about the woman my eyes now frantically sought.

Jinx had entered Club Nexus with her friend, and business partner, Ivy Granger. Granger was a dangerous enough companion, but Jinx's decision to enter the fae nightclub was nearly suicidal. Faeries and vampires both enjoy the diversion of a winsome human and Jinx was an absolute vision of beauty.

Lucifer's pointy pitchfork, what is wrong with the woman?

I gripped my walking stick in a stranglehold until my eyes fell on Jinx and her psychic detective friend seated at the bar. I hurriedly made my way down the stairs, slowing only as I crossed the dance floor. I licked my lips, shivering in anticipation.

I'd come here to ensure the woman's safety, but now that she was within reach, I was overcome with the need to feel her touch—even if I'd have to settle for a crossbow bolt through the chest. One gloved hand drifted to my side where I'd recently received the sharp end of a letter opener. Jinx was nothing if not feisty.

I sauntered to the bar, smiling when Jinx caught my hungry gaze. For a startled moment her face was an open book and her expression mirrored my own. Desire smoldered in her eyes as she absently stroked the crossbow at her shoulder.

"Hello, sweetheart," I said, slipping an arm around her shoulders. "Buy you a drink?"

BURNING BRIGHT SNEAK PEEK

Keep reading the award-winning Ivy Granger series.

Burning Bright (Ivy Granger #3) by E.J. Stevens

Now Available

Trade Paperback . Ebook . Audiobook

CHAPTER 1

Ever play whack-a-mole with a jincan? No? Well, then aren't you the fortunate one. Not only do jincan look like overgrown caterpillars with pointy teeth, but they also breed like bunnies and have a knack for undermining integral weight-bearing structures, leaving piles of rubble in their wake. Oh, and they smell like rotten eggs when squished—just my luck.

I scanned the cratered parking lot and sighed. Ever since Jenna was shipped off to Europe on some top-secret Hunters' Guild mission, Harborsmouth's supernatural pest problem had grown out of control. Jenna was one of the youngest members in the Harborsmouth Guild office and, as such, was responsible for the less desirable hunting jobs—like taking care of a nest of jincan. Now that she was gone, that job fell to the private sector.

I tightened my grip on the iron hammer and scowled. With Jenna gone, and the Guild in no hurry to find a replacement, jobs had come rolling in. I guess I should have been happy for the work, but no amount of money would make this feel like a real case. These jobs were just trumped up pest control. I'd much rather be working a case that required more than whacking some creature over the head. Better yet, I wanted more time to focus on the search for my father.

I'd recently learned that I was half-fae and that my deadbeat dad was Will-o'-the-Wisp, or Willem as my human mom knew him, King of the Wisps. Most of my life I'd spent feeling abandoned by the guy, which pissed me off. My psychic abilities had labeled me as a freak and an outcast, relegating me to the sidelines where I watched other people live their safe, happy, normal lives. Even my mother and step-father had distanced themselves from their freak daughter. To say I had abandonment issues was an understatement.

Imagine my surprise when I discovered, in a search for answers about my awakening wisp abilities, that my dad had been a victim too. He'd been tricked by a demon, possibly

Lucifer himself, to carry a cursed lantern that brought disasters wherever he walked the earth. In an attempt to keep me and my mom safe, Will-o'-the-Wisp had left Harborsmouth. Now I not only needed to find my father, I desperately wanted to.

But time was running out. As if my psychic gift and second sight weren't bad enough, I was growing into a whole new set of wisp abilities that I had no idea how to control. And fae who can't keep their supernatural side hidden from humans don't have a long lifespan—even for immortals. If I don't find my father soon, I'll be facing a fae firing squad. In fact, I could already feel the chill of fae assassins breathing down my neck.

Yeah, sorting out my family issues and finding a way to control my wisp powers should have been my one and only task, but information doesn't come cheap. It takes money to grease those kinds of gears, hence my jumping at the chance to fill the void that Jenna had left in her wake. Jobs like these paid in cash and favors, both of which were in short supply since beginning my search for answers.

As it was, I was accruing debt with the wrong people. Take, for example, my debt to the vampire master of Harborsmouth. I'd promised to work one case of that pompous, old dust bag's choosing. Yeah, that was bound to go well. As if that wasn't bad enough, I'd made not one, but two faerie bargains with The Green Lady. I just knew the glaistig would be calling in her favors soon. I'd caught her guards watching me more than once. I knew she was keeping tabs on her investment and that scared me worse than the threat of faerie assassins.

Unfortunately, the vamp and the glaistig weren't the only ones I'd made bargains with over the past few months. Their bargains were just the most likely to result in death or insanity. By comparison, my alliance with Sir Torn and the local *cat sidhe* was a walk in the park. And that was saying a whole lot about just how potentially deadly my bargains with The Green Lady and the vampire master of the city really were. Torn was a shadowy, feline, pain in my ass who obviously thought my roommate and business partner was catnip—like I didn't have enough to worry about.

One of the caterpillar creatures burst up through a pile of rubble to my left and, with a blur of writhing golden fur, ducked inside the ruins of a video store. Damn, these things were fast. I ran toward the alley at the back of the store, hoping to corner the jincan before it escaped back into the ground or into the multi-level parking garage. Chasing the jincan around in that warren of concrete and steel was something I'd like to avoid. There were fae who liked to inhabit those shadows and I'd rather not come toe to toe with any of them.

I gulped air as I came around the back of the building, scanning the area around the dumpster and metal exit door for signs of the jincan. No eight foot caterpillar here. Maybe I'd been wrong to think it would come this way. Heck, it could be tunneling through the shop floor this very moment. In fact, I could hear a rhythmic thud coming from inside. Crap, I wouldn't collect my fee if I let this critter slip away.

I spun on my heel, ready to sprint back down the alley when a furry steam-train came barreling through the cinderblock wall. The owner of the strip-mall wasn't going to be happy. There was hardly anything left of the place. Too bad I had more to worry about than pissing off my clients.

I needed to stay alive.

A chunk of concrete whizzed past my head and I ducked into a crouch. I blinked away the dust and debris that filled the air and honed in on the creature's location. There, it was halfway through the wall, its head already dipping into the parking garage.

"Oh no, you don't," I said. "Hey, Goldy, over here!"

The jincan raised its head and gnashed its large, brown teeth. Oh yeah, that's attractive. These critters could use some serious dental care.

With a bellowing cry it lunged toward me. I jinked to the right, avoiding those nasty teeth with a few feet to spare. As the creature's momentum carried it forward, I lifted the hammer, bringing it down at the base of its skull. Do caterpillars even have skulls? Whatever, the blow stopped the deafening chomp of its teeth—too bad it also squished the thing's head like a water balloon.

Smelly jincan goo hit me square in the face, on bare skin. I froze, hammer locked in unmoving gloved fingers, as a vision held me rigid in its icy grip. I tried to calm my breathing and ride it out. It wouldn't do me any good to fight it, and I needed to get this over with. If another jincan came along while I was imprisoned by the goo-induced vision, I'd be getting an up close and personal look at those rotting, pointy teeth.

I'd be caterpillar food for sure.

In fact, it looked like I'd be fed to this guy's queen if he had any say in the matter. Oh, goody.

Psychometry is a funny thing. If a strong psychic imprint is made on an object, then someone with my rare gift can read the information that's left behind. In this case, the caterpillar goo was giving me a vision whammy that made my stomach churn. This jincan had three images playing on a compulsive loop and the message of what drove the beast was clear. He wanted to kill, eat, and mate—not necessarily in that order.

And, oh boy, the gal he wanted to impress was a golden-skinned, furless grub the size of a semi truck. *Protect the Queen, feed the Queen, and mate with the Queen.* Oberon's eyes, I needed brain bleach.

Oh yeah, this vision was no joyride—they never were—but visions of jincan males lining up to hump their gelatinous queen? That was sure to give me nightmares. Damn that shit was nasty.

I gagged and shook off the last of the vision. Psychometry is a bitch of a psychic gift, but the thing is, sometimes it comes in handy. Now I knew how to stop these creatures from destroying another city block, even if it was out here in the suburbs. I just needed to squash their hive leader, and I knew right where to find her.

Aware of the gathering gloom, I sprinted into the parking garage. For the second time today, I wished that Jenna hadn't pissed off the Guild and got herself shipped off to Europe. This was one job where I could use some backup. The obese hive leader didn't seem like much of a threat—heck, she looked like a pulsating marshmallow—but I was pretty sure the masses of horny jincan males I'd seen in my vision weren't about to welcome me with open arms, even if they did have about twenty extra sets of the damn things.

I sighed and ducked into the parking garage as the first stars appeared in the darkening sky above the alley. It was going to be a long night.

BIRTHRIGHT SNEAK PEEK

Keep reading the award-winning Ivy Granger series.

Birthright (Ivy Granger #4) by E.J. Stevens

Now Available

Trade Paperback . Ebook

CHAPTER 1

I grimaced at the noodles currently taunting me with their salty broth and rubbery texture, and pushed the steaming bowl away with gloved hands. My stomach growled, but I ignored its rumbling and grabbed a mug of coffee instead.

"Girl, if you keep drinking that sludge without any food in your stomach, you're just asking for total coffee rot gut," Jinx said, leaning a hip against the counter and pointing a red lacquered fingernail my way. "Eat your dinner."

Jinx wasn't my mother, but sometimes she acted like it. Normally, I put up with her bossiness without too much grumbling. Well, maybe some grumbling, but when it came to eating, I usually did what she said. Jinx was my best friend, which was why we were roommates and business partners.

Until recently, Jinx was also the only person in my life who cared if I lived or breathed—or so I'd thought. So when she fussed over me, I secretly felt all warm and fuzzy inside. I wasn't a touchy feely person, being saddled with the curse of psychometry made sure of that. Over time, objects, including people, collect psychic residue and all of those strong emotions—mostly traumatic—sit there just waiting for someone like me to reach out and make contact.

So normally, that meant I ate what Jinx put in front of me, no questions asked. Not today. If I had to eat one more bowl of ramen or plate of mac and cheese, I'd puke.

"I'd rather wrestle with a smelly, pulsating jincan queen," I muttered.

"Well, you won't be wrestling with the fae anytime soon," she said. "Not with you being dead and all."

I sighed, and glared at the bowl of ramen noodles, but ignoring Jinx didn't make what she said any less true. As far as the fae were concerned, I was dead. Last month, the faerie courts sent their assassins, the Moordenaar, to terminate me as my punishment for crimes against the fae. It was against fae law to go around letting the general public know about the existence of Otherworlders.

Faeries are immortal, but they can still be killed if the human masses became aware of the monsters in their midst and decide to take up arms against them. It was why the ability to glamour ourselves was so important.

So when it came to the faerie courts' attention that I was breaking their law, intentionally or not, they ordered my execution at the hands of the Moordenaar. The Moordenaar are very, very good at their job. They'd shot poisoned arrows into my heart, kidney, and liver, and then left me to die.

Humphrey was one of the reasons my assassins hadn't waited to witness my death, and therefore weren't around when my friends force fed me a magic apple that brought me back to life. I'd have to thank him for that someday, though I didn't like the idea of being in a gargoyle's debt. Talk about a rock and a hard place.

"Fine, I'll make you a box of mac and cheese," she said, rolling her eyes. "But just so you know, we're out of milk and butter. It's probably going to taste nasty."

"No, don't waste it," I said. "I'll eat the mac and cheese tomorrow."

I had no intention of eating another box of the stuff tomorrow, or ever, but Jinx didn't know that. Mab's bones, I'd rather starve.

"I have a protein bar in my bedroom," I said with a one armed shrug.

"That's not dinner," she said, eyes narrowing.

"Neither is this," I said, pushing the bowl farther away. "You want it?"

Jinx stared at the bowl, lip twitching.

"Hells to the no," she said.

I snorted, and shook my head. Jinx had been oohing and ahhing over her meals all week, but she was just as sick of ramen as I was. My best friend was tricksy like that.

"Sparky!" I yelled. "You hungry?"

The little demon came tearing out of our bathroom, streaming toilet paper from his long ears, and climbed the rungs of the barstool beside me. With a gleeful squeak, he hopped onto the counter and danced a squirmy little jig.

"Yes, yes, yes, yes!" he sang.

I reached for the package of plastic cutlery we kept on hand for Ceff—my boyfriend the local kelpie king—but Jinx shook her head.

"Wait," she said. She narrowed her eyes, and aimed a ladle at Sparky. "What have you been up to? Have you been playing in the toilet again?"

Forneus claimed that Sparky would someday grow to become a massive demon lord, but that was hard to believe. The little guy was the size of a potbellied Chihuahua and got into just as much mischief. Last week he'd started tossing "treasures" into the toilet to be salvaged by Sparky the great spelunking explorer. Unfortunately, one of those treasures was Jinx's toothbrush.

"Nooooo," he said.

He blushed and gave Jinx a shy smile.

"Then how did you get toilet paper strung up in your ears like garland?" she asked, reaching over to pluck the paper from his ears.

"No toilet, silly," he said. "Trash can!"

I rubbed a gloved hand over my face, and tried not to laugh. Sparky had found the wonders of the bathroom trash can. Oberon save us all.

"Oh my God, ewww!" Jinx squeaked, dropping the toilet paper as if it scorched her fingers.

"Ewww!" Sparky yelled, smiling as he parroted Jinx.

"If it's anything like his game with the toilet, he was probably putting the toilet paper into the trash can, not the other way around," I said. "The toilet paper is most likely clean."

It also meant that he'd probably been adventuring inside the trash can, sifting through who knows what with his bare hands. Apparently, Jinx had come to the same conclusion.

"Go wash your hands," she said, pointing to the bar sink. "And no more playing in the bathroom."

"Then food?" he asked.

"Then you can eat Ivy's ramen noodles," she said. "Now hurry up, before they get cold."

Sparky skipped over to the sink. He leaned out to turn on the faucet and pretty soon he was playing under the running water as if running through a lawn sprinkler. Jinx scowled at the mess the demon was making of her kitchen, but I shook my head and smiled.

"Let him have his fun," I said. "We can always heat the ramen up again later."

"You shouldn't feed him all that salt," she said. "If he were a dog, he'd have hypertension by now."

I shrugged. The kid looked fine, not that I could tell if he had high blood pressure or not. His skin was always tinged red.

"He's a demon," I said. "That food will probably kill us before it does anything to him."

I eyed the bowl of ramen as if it were about to reach out its noodle tentacles and attack.

"If you want to eat real food again, we have to start making some money," she said. "Either that, or we dip into the emergency fund. Oh wait, we can't do that. Someone already spent it."

I sighed. She wasn't entirely wrong to be angry with me, but I hadn't had a choice.

"You know I have to find my father," I said. "He's the only hope I have of gaining control over my wisp powers and clearing my name with the faerie council."

Until I could prove that I wasn't a walking menace to fae society, I had to remain dead. Something we soon discovered meant a huge blow to our income. It's hard to work cases when you're supposed to be six feet under the ground.

"Let me start taking cases," Jinx said. "I can do the leg work, and you can consult from home. If I need your magic touch, I know where to find you."

I shook my head, and waved my hands.

"No way," I said.

"Look, I'll just meet with the clients and get the deets on the job," she said. "If I wear faerie ointment, I'll be able to see if they're not human."

The ingredients to make faerie ointment were expensive. If Jinx was willing to use up the last of her ointment, I knew she was serious about landing a job. That made arguing with her that much more difficult.

Not that I was willing to give up yet. What Jinx didn't know, what I was forbidden to tell any human, was that I had a key to one of the secret gates to Faerie. The only pathway to that gate revealed itself on the summer solstice—a date that was fast approaching. If we took a job now, I'd only be able to help work the case for a few more days. After that, Jinx might be without backup, permanently.

"Faerie ointment doesn't work on the undead," I said.

Vampires have their own glamour, one that faerie ointment doesn't penetrate. I let out a deep, gratifying sigh. I was sure to win this fight.

"I'll only do business during the day," she said.

Crap. I hadn't thought of that. I cleared my throat, trying to think of another reason my best friend shouldn't put herself at risk. I was pretty sure that telling her "food is highly overrated" wouldn't work.

"It's dangerous," I said.

She lifted her chin, eyes shining, and shoulders back and leaned toward me, her palms spread out on the counter.

"Let me do this," she said. "Please."

Damn it. I slumped forward, and put my head in my hands. It was the "please" that did it. Over the past month, Jinx had been trying to prove that she was the same tough-as-nails woman she was before her attack. The fact that she'd show any sign of weakness now, proved how much this meant to her.

"Okay, fine," I said. "But I'm not letting you do this alone. No meeting with clients without me."

We'd have to work overtime to meet my solstice deadline, but it wasn't like I hadn't worked a case round-the-clock before. So long as Jinx kept pumping me full of coffee, we might wrap up a job before I did my disappearing act.

"You can't come to the office," she said with a frown. "It's too dangerous."

"Then I guess, I'll just have to make sure nobody sees me," I said.

SHADOW SIGHT SNEAK PEEK

Go back to the beginning with book 1 in the Ivy Granger series.

Shadow Sight (Ivy Granger #1) by E.J. Stevens

Now Available

Trade Paperback . Ebook . Audiobook

CHAPTER 1

Spectral light shone along my skin as I walked past the sideboard mirror. I hesitated, uncertain where the light was coming from. Raising a small, pudgy hand to my cheek, I stared back at the ghoulish reflection mimicking the motion. There was no ghost, only my own face staring back at me. Looking up and down the hallway, I spied the source of the unearthly glow.

It was only waning moonlight coming in from the skylight overhead. I released the gasping breath I'd been holding and tried to shrug. I had walked this hallway so many times that I'd worn a path down the carpet runner. I was safe in my home. There was no reason to be frightened.

It was a normal school day. My mom and stepfather were still asleep in their bed and I had to rush through my breakfast if I wanted a chance at the bathroom. I tiptoed past the narrow table with bowed legs that held a stack of mail and a porcelain dish overflowing with keys and loose change. I'd grab money for my lunch on the way back to my room.

I poured myself a bowl of cereal and filled my cat's dish with fresh food. Fluffy had been missing for six days, nearly an entire week. We let her roam around the neighborhood during the day, but she had always turned up at the kitchen door in time for her dinner. When she didn't come home before dark, I knew something was wrong. Fluffy was a huge cat who loved her food, she'd never willingly miss a meal.

I opened the back door and rattled the food in her dish, but Fluffy didn't appear. Setting the dish back on the tile floor, I decided to get my chores out of the way while my cereal got nice and soggy, the way I liked it. I lifted a full bag of garbage from the kitchen bin, tied it, and trudged out through the kitchen door.

It had rained during the night and the back steps were damp, but I didn't have far to go. The metal trash bins were kept lined up like suits of armor behind my stepfather's tool shed. I skipped across a patch of wet grass, dragging the bag of garbage. Fireflies lit my way, the sun still hovering along the horizon.

Halting at one of the empty bins, I reached out to lift the lid. My hand touched cool, damp metal and I let out a mew of terror as a series of images burst behind my eyes. It was like being trapped inside a disturbing movie—forced to watch, but helpless to do anything to stop the things you see happening. No matter how badly you want to change events, they continue to roll on before your eyes.

I didn't know then, what I know now. Maybe that's a good thing. Back then I still had hope. Hope that I was dreaming and the nightmare would soon be over. Hope that I had a fever and mom would make everything better. Hope that I just had an overactive imagination. I swore to never watch a scary movie again. It didn't help. Nothing did.

Nothing ever does.

In the vision, my parents' car backed down our driveway just as something loped behind them. The old Buick stopped quickly, but it was too late. My stepfather climbed out to discover he had run over something small and black. In horror, I watched him retrieve a towel from the car and wrap my dead cat into a small bundle that he carried across the lawn to his shed, where he placed her inside the trash bin.

Squeezing my eyelids shut, I screamed.

There are some truths better left unknown. The white lie that Fluffy was missing, maybe just on some grand cat adventure, had been a kindness. The vision of her death was not something a child should ever have to see.

I was having the dream again.

Not just any dream, but The Nightmare

The screaming in my head was useless. The events of the dream were driven by memory, and you can't change the past, no matter how hard you try.

Psychometry is a nasty gift. Unfortunately, it's not the kind of gift you can return for store credit. Lucky me.

*****

"Ivy, wake up," Jinx said. "You're going to be late for work."

"Five more minutes," I muttered.

"No way," she said.

I cracked my eyelids open to see my roommate with both hands on her hips. Crap. She looked serious.

"Tired," I whined, pulling a pillow over my head.

The Nightmare always left me feeling exhausted. I don't think adult bodies are equipped to deal with childhood terrors.

"Nope, nada, not going to happen," she said, deftly slipping the pillow from my sleep-weak grip.

"Come on, Jinx," I said. "Five more minutes."

Jinx was the most unlucky person that I had ever met. She never won anything, and if she bought a lottery ticket, they usually, accidentally, charged her extra. Jess, or Jinx as everyone called her, was known for falling ass over tea kettle for no reason whatsoever. When we first moved into our loft apartment, she tried hammering a lucky horseshoe above the kitchen alcove. It fell on her head, leaving a nasty bruise and a gash requiring six stitches. Since then, we set ground rules. No hammers or other dangerous carpentry tools for Jinx, ever.

Using her nickname only made Jinx more determined. She yanked back the covers, letting a gust of chill morning air do its work. I was out of bed, in the time it takes to bolt upright and gasp, and running for a hot shower. No matter that Jinx had been there first. After a year of living together, I knew that Jinx would always have the bad luck of a cold shower whether I hopped in first or last. She really was the unluckiest chick on the planet.

Fortunately for me, she could still make a mean cup of coffee.

After my hot shower, I slunk slow as molasses to slump onto a bar stool across from Jinx. She slid a steaming mug across the counter that separated the kitchen from the living room. Mmmmm, good and strong.

"You're welcome," Jinx said.

"Thanks," I said. "So why the rush?"

"You have a client in an hour," Jinx said. "I told you yesterday, but you were working a case. I knew you'd forget."

A lot had happened since the day I had my first vision. I wasn't the same innocent kid who believed everything her parents told her and wore little blue stars and pink hearts glued to her sneakers.

Yes, I remember what shoes I was wearing that day— just before I threw up all over them. Some memories stick with you. After gulping air, and crying for my dead cat, I pulled off those cute little kid shoes and tossed them away, along with my innocence and the person that I had been. I dropped my soiled sneakers into the same trash can that had delivered the cruel gift that Fate had bestowed on me. The kid who walked the garbage out that morning had been full of smiles and dreams. The haunted girl who scurried back to the house moved with careful steps, arms hugging herself, a tiny object in motion dreading the simple sense of touch—and the horrors that could now come with it.

I went from being a carefree kid to an introverted loner. I didn't like to be touched and the prospect of handling anything new to me filled me with dread. Have you ever watched a kid pass out in terror when they see a dodge ball coming their way? Okay, maybe you have. But I would shy away from a shared pencil, passed papers, and would totally wig out if I had to sit at a new desk. So I became the school freak. Junior High sucked. High School wasn't much better.

Being a loner left me time to do some research and experiment with my gift. It was during one of those experiments that I met Jinx. Like I said, she's really unlucky. No one should have walked in on me that day. I know I locked the door. Nobody should have seen me holding an old brass compass and writhing on the floor. Not a soul.

I knew from searching the internet that my gift was called psychometry, the supernatural ability to see events, usually traumatic, in an object's history. Jinx taught me how to use my gift to help others. With her help, I started working small cases. Jinx has the people skills and I have the raw talent. Together, after a lot of trial and error, we opened Private Eye, our own psychic detective agency.

Private Eye may sound goofy, but the sign kicks butt. Our friend Olly did the artwork, a graphic of a detective wearing an old-style hat with a third eye emblazoned across his forehead. It probably helps business that we get a lot of repeat customers too. I mean, there are some people who think I'm a crackpot or charlatan, but people who come to us for help, and don't run away, usually feel that our fee is money well spent. Like the guy I had been helping yesterday.

I tried not to shudder. I didn't want to spill my coffee. That case was creepy. Trust me. If I think a case is spooky, then it is beyond weird.

I wasn't surprised that I forgot Jinx telling me about a new client. Handling certain objects was especially difficult and left my mind in a fog. After telling yesterday's client what he needed to know, and collecting my fee, I had climbed the stairs to our loft and crawled into bed. I didn't even wake up to eat dinner with Jinx.

My stomach growled as the realization hit that I hadn't eaten anything since breakfast yesterday. Jinx laughed and passed me a slice of toast slathered in strawberry jam. She totally rocked.

Not only was I eating a delicious breakfast and washing it down with strong coffee, I didn't even have to touch the jam jar or bread bag. Bonus. You never know who has handled the wrapping and under what circumstances. All it takes is for a fat man to brush past the jam jar as he's having a heart attack and I end up gasping over my toast like a fish out of water. It's not fun and not good for the appetite either. Jinx is always trying to get me to eat more and removing food wrappers is one of her new tricks.

"So who is our client today?" I asked. "Anyone I know?"

"Don't think so," she said, drumming ring covered fingers along her coffee mug. "He's not an old client. I checked."

"Any idea what he wants?" I asked.

"Just the unique services of Ivy Granger, psychic detective," she said, waggling her eyebrows. "But he was cute."

"Well, now I know why you forgot to ask," I said.

"My brain did turn to mush for a second," she said, winking. "He's total eye candy. Tall, nice smile, and when he turned around..."

"Okay, I get it, he's super cute," I said, rolling my eyes. "Did Mr. Hottie have a name?"

"That's the weird thing," Jinx said, frowning. "You know how organized I am, right?"

More like totally, obsessively, anal retentive. Her appointment book was her bible. No joke.

"Yes," I said.

"Well, somehow I forgot to put his name in the book," she said, blushing. "I just noted that you had an appointment. Plus, I know he gave me his name because I punched his name into the system to see if he was a former client. The database came up blank."

"Kind of like your brain," I said.

"Exactly like my brain," she said. "Weird, huh?"

"Freaky," I said.

What was really bizarre was the way Jinx bit her lip instead of rebutting my last few comments. I had totally baited her with the "like your brain" remark. She must be really worried about her lapse in memory.

"Maybe you need to take some gingko," I said.

The Chinese herb was used for improving memory, though I was sure my friend's memory was just fine. She just had trouble concentrating when hot guys were in the room.

"Damn, you know I always forget to take it," Jinx said, hitting her forehead with the heel of her hand.

It was an old joke and we laughed as I rinsed my dish in the sink and gulped the last dregs of my coffee. Too bad I didn't have time for another cup. I had a feeling this was going to be a very long day.

*****

I pulled on leather bike gloves, grabbed my keys from the dish by the door and left the loft, waving goodbye to Jinx on the way out. Heat blasted me as I stepped into the stairwell that led down to the street. The stairwell always smelled old, a stratosphere of building history. August heat brought out the scent of curry, vegetable soup, unwashed bodies, tobacco, fabric softener, mildew, and old wood—a pungent olfactory picture, like a patchwork quilt that each tenant contributed to over the years.

I loved our loft and office space. Fortunately for me, nothing really bad had ever happened here. Ever go apartment hunting and wonder, if walls could talk, then what would the walls of this place say about its past? Well, in my case, they can. All I have to do is pull off my gloves and place my hand against the plaster and wood. If something bad happened here, I would know about it. A stinky stairwell was something a girl could get used to. Nightmare visions? Not so much.

I took the steps two at a time, boots clomping against the hollow wood. Another reason to like this place—it was difficult to sneak up on Jinx and me. Not that I was especially worried, but it didn't pay to take any chances. I knew the monsters that walked these streets. Not all of them were human—another little treat that my psychic gift had given me.

As if the horror of seeing death and injury wasn't enough, my special sight also cuts through the veil of glamour that many fae wear...to show the true monstrous visage beneath. Why? Again, I say, Fate is a fickle bitch.

So, yes, I'm aware of the monsters that walk the streets of our city and have taken measures to stay safe. The old, iron lock on the front door was just one of those measures, but an important one all the same.

Turning the key to the right with a solid click, I slid it out of the lock and into my back pocket. From the front of my jeans, I dug out a small packet of salt blended with herbs which I sprinkled along the door sill.

Yes, Jinx would be coming down in about five minutes to make a run to the bank so our rent check wouldn't bounce. And yes, she would relock the door and sprinkle the same combination of herbs and salt along the bottom of the door. Were we over cautious? Perhaps, but this was our home and damn if we'd let some creature-feature nasty just waltz in. I'd *seen* what these things looked like. Trust me. They wouldn't make pleasant house guests.

No, some of the things that lurked in the shadows preferred human flesh, and they were so not getting a taste at this address. I was not coming home to a big baddy picking its teeth with my furniture after having my roommate for dinner. Not going to happen.

Finishing up my ritual, I turned to our office window. I didn't have to go far. The door to our loft was about fourteen inches away from our office. The location was another bonus to living here. I loved this place.

When Jinx found us the cool digs and the incredible office space downstairs, I jumped at the chance. It was a million times better than living at home with my parents. Living with Jinx meant being able to unburden myself of the guilt I always carried back home.

Why the parental guilt? Good question. After four years of intense therapy, I had a perfect macaroni Jesus (I liked to use our art therapy sessions to make religious icons out of pasta. It totally freaked out my therapist), but only an inkling of why I felt so bad about my relationship with my folks. I guess I figured it must be tough to have a daughter who started screaming and drooling when you handed her a birthday present, Christmas gift...or the mail.

Being around my parents and their wary, anxious looks, made me feel guilty. Jinx made me feel important—wanted, needed. Over the years, she had taught me how to be a human being again. Jinx saved me. Not only did she help to give my life purpose by coaxing me to use my gift to solve mysteries, and help people, she also saved me from myself. Jinx did the one thing that my parents, and kids at school, couldn't do, the thing even I hadn't been able to do since I was nine years old. Jinx accepted me for who I was—creepy supernatural gift and all. I totally loved her for that.

Jinx was also an amazing office assistant. Just don't call her my secretary. It pisses her off. Jinx usually runs interference at the front desk, greeting clients and preparing them for my brusque demeanor and touch phobia. She would have been there now, but we were behind on rent. She had to make that bank deposit this morning or we'd be in big trouble with our landlord. I'd have to face the hot mystery client alone. If I didn't know better, I'd think Jinx set the whole thing up. She liked to play cupid. You'd think she'd learn.

With a sigh, I looked at my reflection in the office window. I've been getting stray white hairs since I was in my teens. No big surprise considering the things that I've seen. It was amazing all my hair wasn't pure white. The white bits were adding up though, and looked weird on a twenty-four year old, so last week Jinx dyed my auburn hair an inky shade of black.

The face that stared back at me still looked like a stranger. I don't think I'll ever get used to the jet black hair. It made my pale skin and unusual, almond-shaped, amber eyes all the more pronounced. I slid on a pair of dark sunglasses, pulled a baseball cap out of my back pocket, and tossed it on my head. I felt less conspicuous, which helped me breathe easier. In my jeans and tank top, I just hoped the client didn't mistake me for a boy. I didn't have Jinx's curves or feminine rockabilly style. I envied her ability to pull off halter dresses, 50's era hair, and bitchin' tats. Even her heavy framed, retro glasses were super cute.

I didn't do cute, especially not first thing in the morning.

"Okay, enough stalling," I muttered to my reflection.

I unlocked the office door and switched on the overhead lights. My eyes scanned the room as the lights came on with little pings and clicks. The phrenology head on the filing cabinet, wearing an old-school fedora, always gave me a start. *Damn it, Jinx, that thing is creepy.* I walked in and shoved the hat down over its eyes. I leapt backward into a low crouch when a pen I'd accidentally knocked rolled off the cabinet and onto the floor.

I wasn't sure why I was so jumpy today, but it wasn't a good omen. I hoped it was just the lingering effects of The Nightmare. We needed today's case to go smoothly.

I walked the entire room, poking into corners and shadows, until satisfied that I was truly alone. We really should clean up some of this stuff. Private Eye was filled with a weird collection of occult items and gumshoe detective memorabilia from old books and film noir.

My partner in crime fighting, or at least in finding Gran's lost cat, had a thing for anything retro. The big black phone on her desk looked authentic, but I knew it was a replica. I had to answer it once and didn't get any nasty visions from last century. I scanned the wall behind her desk and grinned. Jinx could totally be one of the actresses featured on the movie posters that papered the wall by her desk—if only those actresses had tattoos and septum piercings.

My desk had its own charm, though *charms* may be more accurate. Over the years, I had researched protection magic. I didn't have any real magic ability myself, other than my second sight, but there were many items that the lay person can use effectively. Herbs, crystals, talismans, protection symbols, I had them all…and most of these were heaped on or around my desk.

It's no wonder we barely had enough money to pay the bills. I spent a fortune each week at Madame Kaye's Magic Emporium, a Harborsmouth landmark run by Kaye O'Shay. Kaye is a sweet old lady, and an incredibly powerful witch. Don't let the tacky shop name fool you. She just plays up her talents for the rich tourists who come in on the ferry each day. Kaye wears more make-up than Jinx, and hovers over a battery operated crystal ball when the day trippers are in her shop, but she's the real deal. I've seen her magic work, which is why I can barely find a place to sit at my desk.

You never know when you'll need a good protection charm. With Jinx's bad luck and my gift for seeing things I probably shouldn't, I was betting we'd need the junk on my desk sooner than later.

I lifted a basket from my chair and set it on top of the metal cabinet beside the phrenology head. A few rowan berries and a piece of stale bread tumbled out onto the floor. That basket of Kaye's goodies could keep a faerie of the Unseelie court at bay. Too bad the Sidhe weren't the only bloodthirsty creatures walking the streets of our city.

I sat back in my chair and waited for my mystery client to arrive.

HUNTING IN BRUGES SNEAK PEEK

Explore the new series within the World of Ivy Granger.

Hunting in Bruges (Hunters' Guild #1) by E.J. Stevens

Now Available

Trade Paperback . Ebook

CHAPTER 1

I've been seeing ghosts for as long as I can remember. Most ghosts are simply annoying; just clueless dead people who don't realize that they've died. The weakest of these manifest as flimsy apparitions, without the ability for speech or higher thought. They're like a recording of someone's life projected not onto a screen, but onto the place where they died. Most people can walk through one of these ghosts without so much as a goosebump.

Poltergeists are more powerful, but just as single-minded. These pesky spirits are like angry toddlers. They stomp around, shaking their proverbial chains, moaning and wailing about how something (the accident, their murder, or the murder they committed) was someone else's fault, and how everyone must pay for their misfortune. Poltergeists are a nuisance; they're noisy and can throw around objects for short periods of time, but it's only the strong ones that are dangerous.

Thankfully, there aren't many ghosts out there strong enough to do more than knock a pen off your desk or cause a cold spot. From what I've discovered while training with the Hunters' Guild, ghosts get their power from two things—how long they've been haunting and strength of purpose. If someone as obsessed with killing as Jack the Ripper manifests beside you on a London street, I recommend you run. If someone as old and unhinged as Vlad the Impaler appears beside you in Târgoviste Romania, you better hope you have a Hunter at your side, or a guardian angel.

The dead get a bad rap, and for good reason, but some ghosts can be helpful. There was a woman with a kind face who used to appear when I was in foster care. Linda wasn't just a loop of psychic recording stuck on repeat; this ghost had free will and independent thought—and thankfully, she wasn't a sociopath consumed with bloodshed. Linda manifested in faded jeans and dark turtleneck and smelled like home, which was the other thing that was unusual about her. Most ghosts are tied to one spot, the place where they lived or died. But Linda's familiar face followed me from one foster home to another. And it was a good thing that she did. Linda the ghost saved my life more than once.

Foster care was an excellent training ground for self defense, which is probably why the Hunters' Guild uses it as a place for recruitment. Being cast adrift in the child welfare system gave me plenty of opportunities to hone my survival instincts. By the time the Hunters came along, I was a force to be reckoned with, or so I thought.

The Hunters' Guild provides exceptional training and I soon learned that my attempts at both offense and defense were child's play when compared to our senior members. I didn't berate myself over that fact; I was only thirteen when the Hunters swooped in and welcomed me into their fold. But learning my limitations did make me painfully aware of one thing. If it hadn't been for Linda the ghost, I probably wouldn't have survived my childhood.

The worst case of *honing my survival skills* had been at my last foster home, just before the Hunters' Guild intervened. I don't remember the house mother. She wasn't around much. She was just a small figure in a cheap, polyester fast food uniform with a stooped posture and downcast eyes. But I remember her husband Frank.

Frank was a bully who wore white, ketchup and mustard stained, wife-beater t-shirts. He had perpetual French fry breath and a nasty grin. It took me a few weeks to realize that Frank's grin was more of a leer. I'd caught his gaze in the bathroom mirror when I was changing and his eyes said it all; Frank was a perv.

Linda slammed the door in his face, but that didn't stop Frank. Frank would brush up against me in the kitchen and Linda would set the faucet spraying across the tiles…and slide a knife into my hand. My time in that house ended when Frank ended up in the hospital.

I'd been creeping back to the bedroom I shared with three other kids, when I saw Frank waiting for me in the shadows. I pulled the steak knife I kept hidden in the pocket of my robe, but I never got a chance to use it. Now that I know a thing or two about fighting with a blade, I'm aware that Frank probably would have won that fight.

I tried to run toward the stairs, but Frank met me at the top landing. Frank reached for me while his bulk effectively blocked my escape. That was when Linda the ghost pushed him down the stairs. I remember him tumbling in slow motion, his eyes going wide and the leering grin sliding from his face.

Linda the ghost had once again saved me, but it seemed that this visit was her last. I don't know if she used up her quota of psychic power, or if she just felt like her job here was finally done. It wasn't until years later that I realized she was my mother.

I guess I should have realized sooner that I was related to the ghost who followed me around. We both have hair the same shade of shocking red. But where mine is straight and cropped into a short bob, Linda's was wavy and curled down around her shoulders. We also share a dimple in our left cheek and a propensity for protecting the weak and innocent from evil.

Linda the ghost disappeared, a wailing ambulance drove Frank to the hospital, police arrived at my foster house, and the Hunters swooped in and cleaned up the aftermath. It was from my first Guild master that I learned of my parents' fate and put two and two together about my ghostly protector.

As a kid I often wondered why Linda the ghost always wore a dark turtleneck; now I knew. Young, rogue vamps had torn out her neck and proceeded to rip my father to pieces like meat confetti. My parents were on vacation in Belize, celebrating their wedding anniversary when it happened. I'd been staying with a friend of my mother's, otherwise I'd be dead too.

I don't remember my parents, I'd only been three when I was put into the foster care system, but I do find some peace in knowing that doing my duty as a Hunter gives me the power to police and destroy rogue vamps like the ones who killed my mother and father. When I become exhausted by my work, I think of Linda's sad face and push myself to train harder. And when I find creeps who are abusive to women and children, I think of Frank.

That's how I ended up here, standing in a Brussels airport, trying to decipher the Dutch and French signs with eyes that were gritty from the twelve hour flight. It all started when my friend Ivy called to inform me that a fellow Hunter had hit our mutual friend Jinx. Ivy didn't know how that information would push all my buttons, she didn't know about Frank or my time in the foster system, but we both agreed that striking a girl was unacceptable. She was letting me, and the Hunters' Guild, deal with it, for now.

I went to master Janus, the head of the Harborsmouth Hunters' Guild, and reported Hans' transgressions. It didn't help his case that he had a reputation as a berserker in battle. The fact that he'd hit a human, the very people we were sworn to defend against the monsters, was the nail in the coffin of Hans' career.

I was assured that Hans would be shipped off to the equivalent of a desk job in Siberia. I should have left it at that, and let my superiors take care of the problem. But Jinx was my friend. Ivy's rockabilly business partner may have had bad luck and even worse taste in men, but that didn't mean she deserved to spend her life fending off the attacks of the Franks in the world.

Hans continued his Guild duties while the higher ups shuffled papers and prepared to send him away. Hans should have skipped our training sessions, but then again, he didn't know who had ratted him out—and the guy had a lot of rage to vent. I stormed onto the practice mat and saluted Hans with my sword. It wasn't long before the man started to bleed.

We were supposed to be using practice swords, but I'd *accidentally* grabbed the sharp blade I used on hunting runs. I didn't leave any lasting injuries, but the shallow cuts made a mess of his precious tattoos. I just hoped the scars were a constant reminder of what happens when you attack the innocent.

One week later, I received a plane ticket and orders to meet with one of our contacts in Belgium. I wasn't sure if this assignment was intended as a punishment or a promotion, but I was eager to prove myself to the Guild leadership. Master Janus' parting words whispered in my head, distracting me from the voice on the overhead intercom echoing throughout the cavernous airport.

"Do your duty, Jenna," he said. Master Janus placed a large, sword-calloused hand on my shoulder and looked me in the eye. I swallowed hard, but I managed to keep my hands from shaking. "Make us proud."

"I will, sir," I said.

"Good hunting."

E.J. Stevens is the author of fourteen works of speculative fiction, including the Spirit Guide young adult paranormal romance series, the Hunters' Guild urban fantasy series, and the award-winning Ivy Granger urban fantasy series. She is known for filling pages with quirky characters, bloodsucking vampires, psychotic faeries, and snarky, kick-butt heroines.

When E.J. isn't at her writing desk, she enjoys teaching writing workshops, dancing along seaside cliffs, singing in graveyards, and sleeping in faerie circles. E.J. currently resides in a magical forest on the coast of Maine where she finds daily inspiration for her writing.

Follow E.J. Stevens on Twitter @EJStevensAuthor

You can learn more about E.J. by visiting her blog
From the Shadows at http://www.FromTheShadows.info

www.ingramcontent.com/pod-product-compliance
Lightning Source LLC
Chambersburg PA
CBHW060632130626
46555CB00002B/772